Ola
Shakes
It Up

Also by
Joanne Hyppolite

SETH AND SAMONA

Ola Shakes It Up

Joanne Hyppolite

illustrated by
Warren Chang

Delacorte Press

Published by
Delacorte Press
Bantam Doubleday Dell Publishing Group, Inc.
1540 Broadway
New York, New York 10036

Library of Congress Cataloging-in-Publication Data
Hyppolite, Joanne.
Ola shakes it up / Joanne Hyppolite ; illustrated by Warren Chang.
p.   cm.
Summary: Nine-year-old Ola and her family are the first black people to move into
Walcott Corners, a stuffy, suburban Massachusetts community that could stand to be
a little bit more like the lively old Roxbury neighborhood that Ola sorely misses.
ISBN 0-385-32235-6
[1. Moving, Household—Fiction.   2. Neighborhood—Fiction.   3. Neighbors—
Fiction.   4. Afro-Americans—Fiction.   5. Family   life—Massachusetts—Fiction.
6. Massachusetts—Fiction.]   I. Chang, Warren, ill.   II. Title.
PZ7.H989701 1998
[Fic]—dc21   97-11718
                                                                                    CIP
                                                                                     AC

The text of this book is set in 11.5-point New Caledonia.
Book design by Kimberly Adlerman

Manufactured in the United States of America

February 1998
10 9 8 7 6 5 4 3 2
BVG

To Joe
('cause if our love is wrong,
I don't want to be right)
and
to Angelique, girl,
thanks for all the support

Chapter One

Operation No-Move

Khatib shut the car door as slowly as he could while Dad tried to start the engine. It made that *err-umph* sound, as if to say, "No way, Jose" (or Brewster, 'cause that's my dad's name), and I knew our old green station wagon felt the same way I did. Then Mama, sitting in the front seat with her thick hair twisted up in a bun so you could see her long, pretty neck the color of almonds, undid all my prayers by whispering, "Oh, Lord," under her breath, and the car started up just like magic. Mama always has her way with God.

Dad turned his head to look at us and smiled his big-teeth smile through his mustache before saying, "We're off," like we were at the races, and the car pulled away from the house that was the only place I'd lived in since I was born. The three of us tried our best to look as sad as possible, 'cause that was the plan. But before long Aeisha was reading one of her books and Khatib was listening to the basketball game on his Walkman and I was the only one left. I was thinking they should have listened to me in the first place, even if I was only nine years old and the youngest, 'cause a good idea is a good idea, and if we'd snuck out the night before and taken the battery out of the car, then we wouldn't have been going to look at our new house in the stupid suburbs right now.

I looked over past Aeisha and out the window to watch as we went up one long hill and down another. Route 128 was all brown hills and trees with no leaves on them, and overhead the sky was thick with gray clouds. Another sign. I looked suspiciously at Dad's freshly cut hair and Mama's new green paisley dress. Why did we have to go to so much trouble to look good just to move someplace, anyway? I was the only one in the car dressed normal, in my favorite jeans and a purple leotard. Seemed like I was the only one in this family who cared that we were leaving a perfectly good home to live in the middle of someplace where we had to dress up before we even moved in.

"Moving?" Khatib had been the first person to speak up when Mama and Dad told the three of us about their big surprise last month. Mama and Dad's news had made him stop thinking about himself for a little while. Ever since Khatib had gotten into high school this year, he thought he was too grown up to hang out with me or Aeisha or the rest of the family. He spent all of his time either at basketball practice or at home on the phone talking to some girl. At dinner or any of our regular family meetings he acted like he was too bored to care about anything we said or did. Mama said it was just a phase he was going through, but I think being in high school had made Khatib think he was God's gift to the world. "Why are we moving?"

"Because we finally got ourselves a chance at buying a house in a nice place—"

"What's wrong with this place?" Khatib asked, looking around the room like he was at the royal palace instead of in our little kitchen with Mama's sewing machine stuck in one corner and the washing machine in the other.

Dad looked real mad that Khatib had interrupted him. His brown eyes got all serious and he pushed his lips together and stayed quiet for a long time, 'cause rule number one in our house is that everybody gets to have their own say—in their own time.

Mama looked down at us from where she was braiding Aeisha's hair and took over. "You all knew that with your dad finishing school and me getting that grant from Walcott College that there were gonna be some changes."

"I thought we were gonna be getting things like new bicycles—not moving," I said. I gave Aeisha, who was humming the theme to an old TV show, a look that said, Help me out here.

Aeisha cleared her throat, finally lowering her book and joining in on this family meeting. "That wasn't made clear to me either."

"You said you probably weren't going to take that grant," Khatib added. His eyes were wide with panic. I knew he was just worried about losing his place on the basketball team. "You said you had better things to do than work for some uppity private college."

"Yeah." All three of us turned to look at Mama accusingly. Mama is a marketing specialist for public health projects. That means people pay her to design ways of getting important medical information to different communities. Mama loves her work even though she's always grumping that it doesn't pay her enough. At Walcott, she wouldn't be working with any communities. She'd be teaching and, as she'd told us, "stuck behind a desk looking over everyone else's projects instead of doing my own."

"This place is too small with all you kids and me and your dad. Moving to Walcott would mean you're all going to get your own rooms." Mama hesitated when she saw that we weren't impressed. Then she looked at Dad, who was sitting with his elbows on his knees, studying the three of us. For a few seconds they stared at each other the way they do when they aren't sure they should tell us something or not. They both looked so different. Dad is tall and thin, with arms and legs that stretch out for miles. Mama isn't fat but she has soft round arms and legs. Khatib, Aeisha and I get our almond color from Mama, but we all have Dad's skinny legs, bushy eyebrows and dark brown eyes.

"Your dad heard back from his interview a few weeks back," Mama said finally.

All of our heads swung toward Dad, surprised. Since Dad had finished taking all his engineering classes, he'd been looking for a job — with no luck. Mama had explained to us that there were very few new jobs open because of the economy, and Boston had even fewer jobs because a lot of companies were shutting down or laying off people. So even though Dad had graduated from night college four months before, he was still working as a mechanic at the ABC garage. He'd been to four interviews already and hadn't gotten

4

one job offer. We all felt bad for Dad, even though he tried to act like it didn't really matter.

"Really?" Khatib asked, for all of us.

Dad nodded, and we all smiled. But before we could hug him or even say congratulations, he spoke up. "But the job's in Earlington — a town over from Walcott."

"Oh." Khatib's face fell, disappointed. He quieted down like he needed to think this over, and I thought it was about time for me, Ola, to put my two cents in and straighten this thing out. "Well, what about Mrs. Gransby?"

"What about her?" Dad asked.

"Is she coming with us?" I asked, planting my elbows on the table. Mrs. Gransby is the Jamaican lady who lived upstairs and took care of Aeisha and me after school. She used to look after Khatib too, but now he has basketball practice after school. Aeisha needs looking after more than I do, even though she's twelve years old, 'cause when she's reading, the house could burn down around her and she wouldn't even notice.

"Mrs. Gransby has her own family, Ola." Dad drummed his long fingers on the table. "You all are old enough to take care of yourselves after school now. But since your mama and I will probably be working more hours, we were thinking about hiring some live-in help."

"A *maid*?" Aeisha asked, raising her eyebrows. "We're getting a *maid*?"

"Not a maid." Mama shook her head. "Some help. Maybe someone young who could use the room and board in exchange for a little housework."

"Sounds like a maid to me." Aeisha shrugged. She took

her glasses off and started cleaning them, which she always does when she's thinking hard about something. Then she looked up again. "Isn't Walcott a white town?"

Aeisha's question left a thick silence in the room.

"How do you know that?" I asked Aeisha finally.

"We had a debate competition there last year." She put her glasses back on.

"Aeisha's right. Walcott is a mostly white area," Mama finally said. She looked at each one of us seriously. "Should that keep us from moving there?"

Aeisha, Khatib and I looked at each other. None of us was sure what to say. It was just like Mama to get right to the heart of the matter. I looked at Aeisha and Khatib and could tell that they both felt the same way I did but didn't know how to explain it. It wasn't that there was something wrong with moving into a white town — exactly. But our neighborhood in Roxbury was all black and Hispanic. We'd never known anything else.

"N-No," Aeisha said at last.

Mama looked at Khatib and me.

"Guess not." Khatib shrugged.

"Well . . . ," I started, hesitating, "it'll just be different." And as far as I was concerned, that was enough reason not to go. Who wanted different when we were perfectly happy right where we were?

Nobody said anything again for a while. Then Mama looked at all of us and smiled brightly. "Walcott is one of the oldest towns in Massachusetts. It was founded in 1712, before there even was a United States of America. Wait till you see it — the town streets have cobblestones, and there's . . ."

Mama droned on and on until she ran out of breath. Then Dad started going on and on about how the new house had two floors, an attic, a big yard and a big kitchen, and how we could get a dog if we wanted, and how Walcott was a town that was full of history. I stopped listening. The only thing I could think of was no Mrs. Gransby waiting for us every day with some plantains and curried goat and West Indian cola. No Mrs. Gransby to cornrow my hair while we watched the soaps together and Aeisha did her homework. And what about my room, which we'd painted white with purple borders for me last year and where we'd put up glow-in-the-dark stars on the ceiling so Aeisha and I could learn the constellations? What about the end-of-the-year recital that my dance class was gonna do at the community center? What about my best friends, Margarita and Karen? We were supposed to go to camp together next summer. We were supposed to learn how to ice-skate this year.

Dad listened to all I had to say, then said we would do good things in the new house and the new neighborhood, too, and that's it, the end, no more discussion, which made me real mad at Dad. What's all this talk about how everybody has their own say in this family for, if it doesn't count for anything? So me, Khatib and Aeisha got together and had our own family meeting. We knew how important this job was to Dad, but our school and our neighborhood here were important, too. Khatib would have to quit the basketball team. Aeisha would lose her record of perfect attendance and I wouldn't be able to go on our class trip to Canobie Lake at the end of the year. Karen, Margarita and I had been looking forward to it since school started.

That's when I decided to come up with a plan. A good plan can solve anything and everything and can get you almost anything you want. And it just so happened that I considered myself to be the best planner this side of Roxbury. I decided that the first thing we needed to do was some research on Walcott. Aeisha found out that there was a commuter train to Earlington and that it would only take Dad four hours each morning to get to work from Roxbury. Aeisha and Khatib thought that was too much, but it didn't seem so bad to me. Dad could get a lot of work done on the train, and when the economy got better he could get a job in Boston. Plus, we knew that Dad felt bad about making us move our whole lives just because of his job. That's how I came up with Plan A of Operation No-Move. First we moped around the house for the whole month, which wasn't too hard to do whenever we thought of having to say goodbye to all our friends. I even told Mama that I thought the psychological ramifications (Aeisha looked that one up for me) of this move on me personally were not worth the risk, but she just laughed. I think I pronounced it wrong. But Plan A was a complete disaster, 'cause instead of letting us stay in our old house, Mama and Dad decided that a visit to the new house would make us feel better about moving. Ha. Luckily, I had a backup plan ready to go.

It seemed like we had been driving for hours by the time Mama said, "We're here," and we all looked out the window to see what here was all about. A big blue sign with a bunch of flowers and birds painted on it announced that we were entering WALCOTT CORNERS: A COOPERATIVE COMMUNITY. Then we were driving on a really wide street that looked like

8

it could fit six lanes of traffic. All around us were gigantic two-story houses with huge brownish green lawns and big, bare trees like the ones on Route 128. The houses all looked the same, with brick stairs that led up to the front door and tall brown fences that went around the sides and the back. It was kind of eerie how organized everything looked. Every house had the exact same football-field-sized lawn and the exact same trees planted in front of it. All of the houses were painted either this sick blue and white or a disgusting peachy pink and white. They all looked like they had been painted yesterday, too. Looking around, I saw that there were no cars parked on the street, like there were in our real neighborhood, and that there was a lot more space in between the houses. It would take a few weeks just to cross the street.

"This place doesn't look very historic," Aeisha commented, frowning against the window.

"That's 'cause this is a new development, Aeisha," Dad said. "All these houses are brand-new."

"It's very unique," Mama added. "In relation to the rest of the town, that is. But it was one of the few places where houses were for sale."

"How come?" I asked suspiciously.

"All the other houses in the town are owned by families that have lived here for generations. People just tend to stay here." Mama smiled brightly again, which made me even more suspicious. I couldn't tell whether she was hiding something from us or just telling us this stuff so that we'd give in and act better about moving. "Wait till you see the inside of the house."

"Where is everybody?" I asked, 'cause there didn't seem

to be anybody outside, though it looked like some stupid kid had left his bike on the lawn across the street. It was definitely too quiet.

"At work or school, Ola. It is a Thursday," Mama answered.

Hmpf, I thought. There was always somebody hanging around in our old neighborhood. If it wasn't Mrs. Petry down the street, then Mrs. Gransby or old Mr. Roland was around to stop you and ask about your family or to make sure you weren't ditching school.

"Which one is ours?" Aeisha asked, pushing her big owl glasses back up her nose. Aeisha's nose is so small that her glasses are always sliding down it.

"Hold your horses, we're almost there." Dad slowed the car down and looked at one side of the street, then the other. "This one," he said, stopping in front of one of the blue-and-white houses. But he didn't open the door. He looked sideways at Mama for help.

"Number seven-twenty-seven," Mama whispered, prodding him to move forward.

"This is number seven-forty-one, Dad," Khatib shouted from where his face was pressed up against the window. He looked back at me and winked, and I nodded, smiling. Aeisha rolled her eyes at us. She thinks my plans are stupid and never work, but what does she know? She doesn't do anything unless she reads about it in a book first. My plans are the kind of thing people *write* books about. Plan B was simple. We had to be as difficult as possible so that Mama and Dad would see that we didn't like the house and would be really unhappy in Walcott.

Dad pulled the car back out into the street, and in a few seconds we pulled into the driveway of another blue-and-white house. "Number seven-twenty-seven. Home."

I stared out of the car window at the house. It made our house back in Roxbury look like a beat-up old shed. This house had big, wide windows instead of the small, tight windows in our old house. This house had a tall, polished wood double door instead of a too-low single door with peeling paint, like our old house. I felt like I was looking at a blown-up-to-life-size version of those dollhouses we used to see in the store catalogs. Aeisha had always wanted one of those dollhouses, but they were too expensive.

Then I looked at the other houses. They looked like dollhouses, too. In fact, they all looked like exactly the same dollhouse. How was I going to find my way home from school in this neighborhood? Even Dad didn't know his own house.

"It's all wrong," I said. Khatib and Aeisha nodded with me. They put on their most sorrowful expressions to show Mama, except that Khatib's expression looked more like he was sick than upset.

Mama twisted her neck to look at us. "It'll look prettier in the spring, when the grass gets back to being green and the trees fill out."

Ha, I thought. What about the humongous front lawn? It looked like it was the size of Franklin Park. Who was gonna take care of it? Dad hated doing yard work and Khatib was always at basketball practice. Who was gonna shovel all the snow in the winter? Who was gonna rake the millions of leaves that fell off those big trees? Not me.

"Come out, all you." Mama held the car door open for me. "At least you can have a look inside."

Khatib, Aeisha and I glanced at each other. I could tell they were wimping out, 'cause neither of them looked me in the eye.

"Guess it wouldn't hurt." Khatib shrugged.

"We're already here," Aeisha pointed out.

"No way!" I whispered loudly.

They looked at each other again, and the next thing I knew they were climbing all over me to get out of the car and running up the front lawn to the house. Traitors.

"Come on out, Ola," Mama coaxed, still holding the door open. "It'll do no good to sit there by yourself."

I decided to get out of the car. Plan B was ruined, anyway. Dad, Aeisha and Khatib had already disappeared into the house. Mama put her hand on my shoulder and we walked up the stairs to the door, which had a big sign with yellow balloons on it that said, WELCOME TO YOUR COOPERATIVE HOME.

"What does that mean?" I asked suspiciously.

"This is a cooperative neighborhood, Ola." Mama opened the door and pushed me inside.

"What does that mean?" I repeated, looking around. We walked down a long hallway into a big square room with white walls and dark wood floors. There was even a fireplace at one end of the room. Dad was standing in front of the tall, wide windows with his hands in his pockets. Everything looked new — like it had never been touched before. Our old house, with its worn-down wood floors and faded yellow-flowered wallpaper, looked more homey.

"It means that everyone in the neighborhood does things to keep it a nice place," Mama explained, going over to stand by Dad. I could see their faces reflected in the window.

"Like what?" This whole cooperative thing sounded fishy to me.

"Like cutting your lawn regularly—"

"Hear that, Dad?" I said, and had to move before his hand reached down to swat my behind for being fresh. "What else?"

"Little things, Ola, like keeping the house in good shape, not parking your car out in the street, not hanging clothes out in the yard—"

"What will they do if you don't do all that stuff?" I asked, but Mama and Dad were smiling at each other, and I decided to get out of there. They were crazy, expecting us to leave our home for this strange place where they had rules that forced you to mow your own lawn. Whose house was this, anyway? The more I thought about it, the more fun I decided it would be to break one of those rules. I could see the headlines: "Nine-Year-Old Ayeola Benson Arrested by Neighborhood for Hanging Out Purple Leotard." If this was really our house— if I thought for a moment that we were gonna stay here—I'd put something out there right now.

I wandered around the house until I found the kitchen. Dad was right— it was much bigger than our real kitchen. It had a long counter with tall black stools, and the tile on the floor was black and green. Off to the side was a little room with our new washing machine and dryer. I went further into the kitchen and looked out the window over the sink. The backyard was even bigger than the front lawn. Someone had cemented part of it and put in a basketball hoop. Now Khatib would never want to leave. I climbed up on one of the stools and sat down.

There were too many corners and too many white walls. Aeisha would be able to find a million places to hide and read her books without me pestering her to come out and live a little. (If it wasn't for me, Aeisha would be the world's only twelve-year-old hermit.) We wouldn't be able to sit together in the kitchen doing our homework while Dad prepared for one of his classes and Mama hummed under her breath. We wouldn't be able to lie down on Mama and Dad's bed all squashed together to watch TV. This house was so big we would never see each other. And nobody in the family was talking about how different it would be for us here. Back in the car I'd seen how Aeisha put down her book and Khatib took off his Walkman to look out the window at the town. They'd been thinking the same thing I was. Walcott was a historic old town, all right. A historic old *white* town. We hadn't seen a single other black or Hispanic face.

Dad came into the kitchen, looked at my long face, and sighed. "Ola, you got to give the place a chance, now."

I shook my head. "It's all wrong for us, Dad. I don't think we should stay here."

"Well, then, what are we gonna do about Grady, huh?" Dad put his hands on his hips and cocked his head.

"Who's Grady?" I asked, but before Dad could answer I heard the barking, and Aeisha rushed into the kitchen leading a big yellow-gold dog with a bright red bow around his neck.

"Look, Ola!"

"A dog!" I shouted, before I could help myself. I jumped off the stool and went to look at him. He had floppy ears and a black nose. I reached out to touch his fur. He felt really soft.

"This is blackmail, Dad," I said, putting my hand behind my back quickly. I looked away from Grady to Dad, who was smiling his big-teeth smile again. We couldn't have any pets in our other house because it was too small.

"A golden retriever, too, Ola," Aeisha added.

I glared at Dad. He was cheating. *I* was the one who always asked for a dog every Christmas. Each year I asked for a different kind of dog to see if maybe that would change their mind. Last year I'd asked for a golden retriever. One year, when I was real little, I'd started crying because they gave me a stuffed dog instead. Dad had hugged me and said he was very, very sorry.

"Now what are we gonna do if we have to go back?" Dad asked. "The pound is keeping him until we move in."

"You got him at the pound?" I asked, kneeling down in front of Grady. I looked into his brown dog eyes. Grady looked back at me and started whimpering. Even the dog was in cahoots with this move.

"An old lady had left him there, Ola." Dad had turned his lips down at the corners, so it looked like he was sad instead of happy. "She said she couldn't take care of him anymore."

"Poor Grady," I said. I couldn't help myself. I had to pat him again.

"Are you ready to give this place a chance now?" I heard Dad ask from behind me. I pulled my hand back quickly. Then I shook my head and stood up.

"He's cute, Dad. Too bad we have to give him back."

But Dad started smiling again, and I left the kitchen to go think about this new development. I knew we wouldn't be able to take Grady back with us. And I knew that Khatib and Aeisha were gonna be useless from now on. They wanted a dog as much as I did.

I started up the stairs. I would go look at the rest of the house while I tried to figure out what to do. Upstairs, there was a wider hallway with more white walls and shiny wooden floors. There were three rooms on each side and a window shaped like an arch at the end. I looked into the first room quickly and found Khatib there, checking himself out in the bathroom mirror.

"There aren't any girls around here but me and Aeisha, you know," I told him, looking around at the bathroom. It had ugly wallpaper with orange and brown dots on it. It also had a separate bathtub *and* shower.

Khatib didn't even look at me. He took his little black comb out from his back pocket and started combing the sides of his hair. "Did you see your room yet?"

"What room?" I asked. "Aeisha probably got the biggest one already."

I waited for Khatib to say something, but he ignored me and started trying out different "cool" looks in the mirror. I rolled my eyes and got out of there quick. Once I'd seen Khatib actually kiss himself in the mirror. He said he was pretending to kiss someone else, but that made me even more sick.

I walked down the hallway and looked at the other rooms. Two were big, square, empty bedrooms. One of them had a window seat in it. Aeisha would love that. The other one smelled like paint and was freezing cold because someone had left the window open. I was starting to think about how to stage my fit when I walked into the third bedroom, which was painted white with purple borders. I stopped and looked up. There over my head was a ceiling full of glow-in-the-dark stars. It was my room.

"Well, what do you think?" I turned around and saw Dad in the doorway, still smiling. Grady was sitting next to him, and for a second it looked like he was smiling, too. I looked at the room for a few seconds, then back at Dad. It was the only room in the house that was decorated special.

"Just a chance, Ola."

I guess Dad *had* been listening to me, a little.

"Okay, Dad." I gave him a hug and swallowed. A four-hour commute did seem a little too much. We would never see Dad. Maybe Mama and Dad were right — maybe this move wouldn't be so bad. Khatib was always saying that I should be more optimistic. But as hard as I tried, I couldn't think of anything worse than being stuck in Walcott.

Chapter Two

Goodbye to Mrs. Gransby

"Aeisha? . . . Aeisha! . . . *Aeisha!*"

Dad popped his head up from behind a pile of boxes and looked at me like something was hurting him bad.

"Ola. You're killing my ears."

"Hmpf," I said, kicking one of the cardboard boxes.

"Ola." This time Dad's voice was sterner, and I looked down at my purple-and-black sneakers. I knew I was gonna get a lecture, and it was all Aeisha's fault, 'cause she was hiding away somewhere reading and I couldn't find her, 'cause there were boxes all over the house and furniture turned upside down like to say, Get out 'cause this ain't your house anymore. And after the weekend, that was just the way it would be. I'd tried to be a good sport about this move for a few days, but seeing everything packed up had brought all my doubts back. It seemed like everything I did was for the last time. My last dance class at the community center had been Thursday. My last day of school had been that day, Friday. And it was also the last time we would see Mrs.

Gransby, because on Saturday she was going to New York to see her daughter Clarisse. To top it all off, Karen and Margarita were mad at me 'cause I was leaving. They said I hadn't tried hard enough to stop it.

"You should have cried and screamed more," Margarita had said. She had dropped her end of the jump rope right in the middle of a song. "You should have had a plan C, D, E and F, and if those didn't work, you should have had a super emergency backup plan."

Then Margarita slapped her hand against her forehead and moaned. She was being very dramatic, as usual, because she wants to be a famous actress someday. She's always talking about how hard it is for Puerto Rican actresses to make it big and so she has to practice, practice, practice all the time.

I sighed and tried telling Margarita and Karen about how I had a backup plan. I had called it Operation No-Sell. I had even tried to get Aeisha and Khatib involved. But Mama and Dad had gotten to them before I could. Khatib found out that Dad had made special arrangements for him to try out for the basketball team at Walcott High School. Dad told Khatib that Walcott's team was in a better league and was undefeated, which was all Khatib needed to hear. He loved the glory of winning. Then Mama told Aeisha that our school had an advanced honors program she would be able to enter, and I knew she would be no help, either.

I had gone on with Operation No-Sell on my own. I had put a sign that read HOUSE QUARANTINED FOR MEASLES: ENTER AT YOUR OWN RISK on the door whenever any real estate people came over to look at our house. When Mama had caught on to that, I started putting big cans of Raid and mousetraps all over the house so potential buyers would think we had roaches and mice. I plugged the sinks and the toilet with paper so they would think we had bad plumbing. I forgot to give Mama phone messages from the realtor who was handling the buying of the new house in Walcott. But I had underestimated Mama and Dad. They found a really old couple named the Martins to buy our house. They were so blind they didn't even see the cans of Raid or the backed-up toilet or the quarantine sign.

"Did you try running away, like I told you?" Karen was still turning her end of the jump rope even though the other end was on the ground. I knew that meant that she was upset, too.

"Aeisha told them before I could even get out the door," I muttered. "Besides, that never works. They know I always go to your house, and your mom always calls them."

"This time she wouldn't have," Karen insisted. She leaned closer to me, and I could see the pale brown freckles on her face. Karen's got skin the color of cinnamon, with freckles so light that you can't see them unless you look close. "I swore her to secrecy."

"You didn't see all the work they did on my new room. They were ready for me." I tried to defend myself. "Aeisha and Khatib finked on me, and then there was Grady. I was outnumbered."

Karen and Margarita didn't say anything.

"We're not moving 'cause we *want* to," I tried to explain. "We're moving 'cause we *have* to. Come on, let's finish playing."

Margarita looked away from me, but she picked up the other end of the rope again. I was hoping that playing our favorite jump-rope game would distract them from my bad news. I jumped into the rope and Karen and Margarita started singing the jump-rope rhyme we'd made up for me last summer.

Mama put cola in my cup
Ola, child, don't shake it up
Mama put braids in my hair
Ola, child, best leave them there

We had made one for each of us that was supposed to show parts of our personality.

Mama made me put on a dress
Ola, child, don't make a mess
Mama told me not to run
When, Mama, will I have some fun?

Listening to the song as I jumped, I started thinking again. Karen and Margarita were right. I couldn't give up so easy. My breath started to come out in pants as they turned the rope faster for the last part.

I wanna shake it up,
            shake it up,
                        shake it up
        Like an earthquake. . . .

At the end of the song, I waved my arms and legs like crazy while I jumped. I was supposed to look like I was in an earthquake, but actually I was just excited. Karen and Margarita and our jump-rope song had helped me come up with another plan.

When Karen and Margarita had said goodbye to me after the game, I could tell how sad they still were. I'd wanted to tell them not to give up yet. I still had one last plan to try, but I hadn't wanted to get their hopes up. This plan called for drastic measures.

"Ola," Dad said again now, to make me look at him.

"Yes, Dad?" He didn't look too mad, just tired. No wonder, with all the packing we'd been doing. Something else was different about Dad's face, too.

"You shaved your mustache off!"

"There's delicate things in some of these boxes. If you kick one, you might break something."

"Don't change the subject, Dad," I said, waving my finger at him. Dad had always had a mustache — for as long as I've been alive. It was thick and black and wavy, and I used to sit on his lap and brush it with one of my doll combs when I was real little. "Why'd you shave your mustache?"

"Ola, I'm not changing the subject. Don't kick any more of these boxes." Dad put his hand up to touch where his mustache used to be. "You don't like it?"

I stared at him. Too many things were changing way too fast around here for me lately. Now Dad had changed his face. "Why'd you do it? Don't they allow mustaches in our corporation neighborhood?"

Dad reached out and tugged one of my braids. "Cooperative. No, Ayeola, that's not it. I just needed a change. New house. New job. No more taking classes at night. This is a good change, Ola baby."

Ah-ha, that's it! I thought. Dad was afraid of looking like an old fogey at his new job. I'd heard him on the phone telling his twin brother, Uncle Louis, that the people at his new job were a bunch of young, hotshot kids who were fresh out of college and who probably didn't even know how to shave yet. Dad had just finished college, too. But he wasn't a kid and it took him six years to get his engineering degree 'cause he had to take classes at night and work too. I looked up at Dad again and saw that his hair was shorter. Another haircut. At this rate, Dad would be bald by the time he went off for his first day at work. He *did* look younger, but it still looked like something was wrong with his face.

"You look younger, Dad," I said, deciding to be nice. "But next time, will you consult me before you make these drastic changes?"

Dad looked like he was trying not to smile, which was just what I wanted. "Yes, Ola."

"Good . . . *Aeisha!*" I screamed, darting out of the kitchen before I could get another lecture. Dad's mustache and us moving weren't the only things that were changing around here. Soon we were going to have a whole other person coming to live with us. Mama had called a family meeting the day before to tell us about it.

Mama had made us sit down around the kitchen table before speaking. "I found someone to help us around the house."

"We don't need a maid, Mama." Aeisha had spoken up,

leaning forward. "Any maid we got would leave after they had to wash Khatib's funky socks, anyway."

"Hey." Khatib dug his elbow into Aeisha's side. "What about you and your dirty feet?" Aeisha hates to wear shoes. She walks around barefoot all the time.

"Come to order," Dad boomed out. He takes these meetings very seriously. "We're not getting a maid."

Mama nodded, her dark brown eyes looking at us intently. "We're going to be helping out someone who can also help us. Marie-Thérèse told me about this girl."

Marie-Thérèse is a Haitian lady that Mama worked with on a project for a community health center last year. They spent almost a year putting together programs and advertising that would educate black women about different cancers. Marie-Thérèse and Mama became good friends after that, and she'd been over all week helping us pack.

Mama was still talking. ". . . she doesn't have any family here and she's lived a very hard life —"

"Where's she from?" I interrupted.

"Weren't you listening, dodo head?" Aeisha raised her eyebrows. "She's from Haiti. She's one of those boat people."

"They let her and a few others into the country because she was sick, and she's been in the hospital for the past five months," Dad said. "Now she's better and she has no place to go. According to Marie-Thérèse, the girl wants to stay here and make a good life for herself. She'd be helping us out at the same time."

"How old is she?" Aeisha asked.

"Twenty."

"What's her name?"

"Lillian."

"Does she speak English?" I asked, remembering Marie-Thérèse's thick accent.

"Some. She needs more practice. She learned some English here and some in Haiti. She's supposed to be very smart." Mama looked at me, then at Khatib and Aeisha. "She needs sponsors to stay in the United States. What do all of you think?"

None of us said anything. I looked around at everybody's faces. Mama and Dad were watching us. I could tell they had already made up their minds to take Lillian, but they were letting us make the final decision. Aeisha looked like she was turning everything that had been said over and over in her mind, and Khatib looked bored. As for me, it was hard to imagine another person living with us. But this person sounded like she needed us more than we needed her.

"We can try," Aeisha said finally, as practical as ever.

But the last thing I wanted to think about was another change while I was still trying to prevent the first one. I decided that this Lillian person would just have to come live with us in our real house in Boston. We could set up a cot for her in the corner of the living room, just like we did when any of our relatives stayed over. She would be nice and comfy there.

I put all my planning skills to work and came up with Operation Obstruction of Justice. Well, actually, I got the idea from watching the news. They had a story about a man who had lost his job unfairly and had handcuffed himself to his desk at work. He said that he wasn't going to leave until they gave him his job back, and it worked. I figured that with a few changes here and there, the same plan could work for me. But first I had to find Aeisha.

After searching up and down for her inside the house, I headed outside to look in one of her favorite hiding places, the garage. I looked through one of the small square windowpanes in the garage door and sure enough, I could see the top of her head from where she was sitting on Mrs. Gransby's old red velvet armchair. I remembered that Mrs. Gransby had had a big fight with her son, Montel, about that chair.

"But I don't want to sell the thing, child," Mrs. Gransby had said in her singsongy accent. The way her voice goes up and down with each word makes it sound like music to me. "It old-old like me — but it don't dead yet. You going to give me away like that?"

I had looked up from the television and watched as Montel sighed and straightened his tie. "Whatever you say, Ma. You the boss lady."

Thinking about that made me remember that Mrs. Gransby was waiting with what she thought was a special last lunch for Aeisha and me.

"Aeisha!" I yelled, rapping on the glass.

Aeisha jumped up like a scared cat and peered over the back of her chair at me. "Go away, Ola."

I walked into the garage. "Whatcha doin'?"

Aeisha gave me a dirty look. "What do you want?"

"You reading? Whatcha reading?" I asked. Aeisha never goes anywhere without a book. She's a hopeless brain.

"Nothing," Aeisha said quickly. Her ears were turning

red. Lately Aeisha's been reading those smoochie teenage romance novels and hiding it, but I know, 'cause I make it my business to know everything that goes on in this family.

"Look what I got." I reached into my pocket and pulled out a pair of plastic handcuffs. They were kid-size.

Aeisha frowned. "Where'd you get those?"

"Thomas and Jose from across the street let me borrow them. Their dad gave them a police game last Christmas." I waved the handcuffs in front of Aeisha.

"Ola, you aren't up to one of your stupid plans, are you?" Aeisha leaned forward. "'Cause it's too late. We already sold the house."

"We gotta go, Aeisha. Mrs. Gransby is waiting." I should have known not to try and share my plans with Aeisha. This time I would show her.

"I didn't forget," Aeisha said, standing up and looking down at her brown feet. She didn't want to say goodbye to Mrs. Gransby, either. Finally, someone in this family was showing a little emotion about moving besides me.

"Come on, Aeisha," I said, grabbing her hand and pulling her out of the garage. We walked around the side of the house to the door that led to Mrs. Gransby's floor of the house. As we headed up the stairs I could smell curry and chicken and other yummy cooking smells, and suddenly I felt like I wanted to cry.

"Well, my young ladies," Mrs. Gransby said as she opened the door for us. She said *ladies* so it sounded like "layties." "But look how they faces set up like rain! No crying before you eat, hear? We just going to act like this any other day you come home from school or from day camp. I even taped our soap so we could watch it together, Ola. That she-witch Delilah about to tell that goody-goody Mariah she carrying her husband's child."

I focused my thoughts on Operation Obstruction of Justice and swallowed my sadness.

"Better. Better." Mrs. Gransby ushered us into the kitchen. She had the table already set, and the stove was covered with pots. "But still not good. What a shame. I really outdid myself cooking for you today. Roti, codfish fritters, juneplum juice. Look like you ladies too sad to eat."

"Chicken roti?" Aeisha asked. I looked at Aeisha and she looked at me, and we both rushed to sit down at the table. Chicken roti is our favorite. It's made of chicken, potatoes, and curry sauce rolled up in a flat round bread. Mama says Aeisha and me are unusual because we like to eat all kinds of food, unlike other kids. But Mrs. Gransby's roti is the best food ever. And I kinda like the idea of being unusual, anyway. If I was a magician, that would be my stage name—Ola the Unusual.

Mrs. Gransby put two tall glasses of juneplum juice in front of Aeisha's plate and my plate. Then she sat down across from us and took a sip from her own glass. I chewed on my roti and watched Mrs. Gransby drink. Mrs. Gransby never ate with us 'cause she's forever on a diet. She thinks she's too big 'cause her stomach has rolls in it and she has to wear a girdle to fit into her dresses. But I think Mrs. Gransby is beautiful. She has such soft, smooth brown skin, the color of chocolate, and big dimples that come out whenever she's laughing. Mrs. Gransby treats us just like her grandchildren, though she has seven to treat nice already.

"I don't know how they going to get along without me at work." Mrs. Gransby shook her head sorrowfully. She had been planning this visit to see her daughter Clarisse for months now.

Aeisha and I nodded. We had our mouths too full to say anything. Mrs. Gransby has a very important job. She's a career counselor for a job training program in downtown Boston. It's up to her to find work for people who really need it. But Mrs. Gransby does more than that. She tries to find the right work for people. She says everyone has native talent for something and it's up to her to make sure the job they get uses their native talent.

"Probably send people with native talent for sewing to job in hotel and people with native talent for writing to job in 'counting," Mrs. Gransby grumbled. She raised a hand and sighed. "I don't want to think 'bout it."

"Mrs. Gransby," Aeisha said, putting down her roti, "in case Mom and Dad didn't tell you, you're always welcome to come and visit us in the suburbs. And if you ever get tired and want to hide out from Montel or your other children 'cause they're bothering you for money all the time, you can come and live with us — permanently."

I nodded hard since my mouth was full of roti. Until my plan could start, I had to act like I was going along with this move.

"You can have Ola's room," Aeisha added, taking a swallow of her juneplum juice. I tried not to choke on my food.

Mrs. Gransby laughed loud, and her dimples flashed in and out. "I may just have to take you up on that, Aeisha. God knows I get tired of them children asking for handouts like they not thirty-forty year old. I'm sure I'd feel like me outside in Jamaica sleeping under all them stars Ola got on her ceiling."

I swallowed the last piece of my roti fast and looked back and forth at Aeisha and Mrs. Gransby. I was never going to live in that room, but Aeisha didn't know that. I wanted to ask her, What's the big idea giving it away without consulting me? But I didn't want to make Mrs. Gransby feel bad.

"Sure, Mrs. Gransby, you can share my new room with me," I said. Under the table, I kicked Aeisha's leg, hard.

"Ow!" Aeisha shouted, glaring at me.

Mrs. Gransby laughed again and stood up. "Don't you worry, Ola. I not going to take you brand-new by-yourself room away from you. But I promise that I visit you before Christmas come."

"Good." Under the tablecloth, I started to slide the handcuffs out of my pocket. I wrapped one handcuff around the chair rung behind me and heard the soft click as it locked. The rest of my family could move to Walcott if they wanted. I slipped one of my wrists into the other handcuff and closed it. I was adopting Mrs. Gransby and staying right here in Roxbury.

"Let's go watch that story now, Ola. After that I have a surprise for both of you." Mrs. Gransby stood up and grabbed one of Aeisha's hands. "Come on now, Ola."

I shook my head. "I can't, Mrs. Gransby."

"You can't what, Ola?"

"Can't come with you," I said. "I can't move."

Aeisha ducked her head under the table and came back up sighing. "She handcuffed herself to the chair, Mrs. Gransby. She's crazy."

"I am not!" If I hadn't been handcuffed, I would have pounced on Aeisha for that.

Mrs. Gransby came around the table to see. She looked at my hands and then back at my face. "Well, Ola, are you going to spend the rest of your days in my kitchen?"

I nodded. "If you don't mind, Mrs. Gransby. I'm adopting you. Mama and Dad will understand."

"That's what you think." Aeisha crossed her arms.

"They'll be sorry they tried to make me move." I shifted a little, 'cause my arm was starting to feel uncomfortable from being pulled behind my back.

"After they kill you." Aeisha turned and dusted off her hands. "Don't pay any attention to her, Mrs. Gransby. Let's go watch the stories."

Aeisha left the room without seeing the horrible face I'd made just for her. Mrs. Gransby was still standing with her hands on her hips. I hoped she wasn't going to try to talk me out of this. Mrs. Gransby is one of the few people in the world who can talk me out of something.

"You know, I don't think this is such a hot idea, Ola chile." She shook her head gravely.

"You don't?"

"Well, it's the timing. You're not moving until Sunday, and your parents won't give in to you so soon as now. No — if I know Brewster and Fatima, they'll let you rot in that chair for two whole days," Mrs. Gransby said very seriously. "Meanwhile, how you going to go to the bathroom? How you going to sleep? What you going to do with yourself when I have to leave for New York tonight?"

I hadn't thought about that. It would be like Mama and Dad to let me stay handcuffed for two whole days just to teach me a lesson. But it would be worth it in the end.

"I can stand it, Mrs. Gransby. Is it okay if I live with you? I know I didn't ask you or anything." I looked at her with my best pleading eyes.

Mrs. Gransby tapped her foot on the kitchen floor. "I tell you what, Ola. I'll just go in there and watch the story with Aeisha for an hour. I'll wait to give you your gifts —"

"Gifts?" If I had known Mrs. Gransby was going to give us presents, I would have waited until after I opened mine to lock myself up.

"I come back to see you in an hour. If you're still feeling that you can stand sitting in that chair with your arm all twisted up for two days, then you can live with me for as long as you like." Mrs. Gransby gave me a big smile and left the room.

I was glad Mrs. Gransby was going to let me live with her, but I wished she hadn't mentioned my arm. It was starting to hurt more. I heard the television come on, and I leaned over as far as I could to listen.

I could stand it.

A little pain was nothing.

It was worth it.

I tried to focus on all the good things about living with Mrs. Gransby. I'd get to eat West Indian food all day long. I'd get to sleep in the living room, where the TV was. I'd be able to help baby-sit all of Mrs. Gransby's grandchildren. But best of all, I knew my family wouldn't survive two weeks without me. Aeisha would fall asleep with her glasses on every night and squash them all up. Mama wouldn't remember what to buy at the supermarket without me there to remind her. Dad would make the family meetings last a whole day without me there to keep him on track. They were gonna fall apart without me around.

My arm wasn't bothering me so much now.

That's because it was totally numb.

Of course, it was also true that my family would have an *easier* time adjusting to Walcott without me there. They'd forget all about the old neighborhood. I wiggled my arm and tried not to yelp. Now it felt like someone was sticking little pins in it. Mama and Dad would be so busy working at their new jobs that they wouldn't have time to think about the million and one reasons why moving to Walcott was the biggest mistake of their lives. I was sure my arm was gonna fall off any minute. Aeisha and Khatib would make new friends and forget about their old ones. They could get so used to *not* having me around, they might forget about how good I was for them.

"Mrs. Gransby!"

Mrs. Gransby and Aeisha ran back into the kitchen. Aeisha was laughing at me, but Mrs. Gransby looked serious. I ignored Aeisha. She didn't know that I had given in just for her and the rest of the family. They needed me. I would find a way for *all* of us to move right back to Roxbury.

"What can I do for you, Ola?"

"You can send Aeisha to Thomas and Jose's house to get the keys for these handcuffs," I said loudly. "My arm hurts."

By the time Aeisha got back, Mrs. Gransby had massaged the feeling back into my numb arm. Aeisha unlocked the handcuffs, and I pulled my arm around and wiggled it. It was okay. It was hard to believe it had been hurting me so bad just a few minutes before. I grabbed Mrs. Gransby's hand and avoided looking at Aeisha. "Come on, Mrs. Gransby. Let's go finish watching our soap."

"Wait. Wait." Mrs. Gransby pulled my hand. "I got to give you all your presents."

Presents! Aeisha and I smiled and started wiggling as Mrs. Gransby took two packages down from one of the cabinets. Presents, and it wasn't even our birthdays.

"This one for you, Aeisha." Mrs. Gransby handed her a square, flat package. I could tell it was a book. "It's about a girl your age name Laetitia who live in Trinidad. And she like roti, too."

Aeisha ripped open the wrapping and took out a book that had a picture of a girl looking out a window at the sea. "Thank you, Mrs. Gransby."

"This one for you, Ola."

I took the long package and ripped the wrapping off fast. I was hoping Mrs. Gransby had gotten me some new ballet slippers or a stuffed pig for my stuffed animal collection or even just one of those big packages of bubble gum.

It was a book. "Thank you, Mrs. Gransby. It's nice."

"You don't even look at it, Ola." Mrs. Gransby smiled, tapping the book. "And I got it special for you."

It's not that I don't like books. I'm not as crazy about them as Aeisha, but I don't mind reading every once in a while. History is my favorite subject at school. But books are the kind of gift you give Aeisha—not me.

I looked at the title politely as Aeisha whispered, "Just what you need."

Ms. Pitapat's Guide to a Perfect Pooch. It was a dog-training book. The cover had a black-and-white picture of a dog balancing three beach balls on his nose.

"I did a little research, Ola, and I'll have you know that Ms. Pitapat is the leading authority on teaching a new dog old tricks." Mrs. Gransby winked. "Circus tricks. Ms. Pitapat trains circus dogs all over the world."

I grinned and hugged Mrs. Gransby around the waist. "You're great, Mrs. Gransby."

Aeisha hugged her, too, and Mrs. Gransby looked down at us and sniffed. "You're welcome, my young ladies."

Chapter Three

Welcome to Walcott

Something was definitely wrong.

I peeked up at the stars on my ceiling and then pulled the covers back over my head.

Yup.

Moving day had been as bad as I hoped it would be, but nobody appreciated it. Not even me. I'd made Mama mad at me, and Aeisha had called me a "first-class brat," and for the first time in my life I'd volunteered to go to bed early. So, here I was. But even that wasn't going right. First of all, it was too quiet in this new room. I couldn't hear if Dad was listening to the jazz station before he went to bed. I couldn't hear any water sounds from the bathroom, and I couldn't hear the sound of Mrs. Gransby's granddaughter running around upstairs because Mrs. Gransby watches her at night. For all I knew, everybody could have left me in this new house all by myself.

Second of all . . . I didn't even want to think about that one.

Third of all, this Lillian person would be coming to live with us anytime now. Mama told us that we'd been approved as sponsors and that Lillian was on her way. I didn't know if I liked the idea of somebody else living with us. She could mess up the way this family works.

Fourth of all, I couldn't shake the feeling that something was really wrong with this neighborhood. The inside of our house was super nice, but the outside of it and all the other houses was like nothing I'd ever seen before. Maybe it was because I was used to houses being older, like they are in Boston. Our real house was built in the 1920s, and in our real neighborhood, all the houses were built in different styles. The houses here were too new and looked too much like each other. The big spaces between the houses made it seem unfriendly here — like the neighbors didn't want to talk or know about each other. I'd sat outside on the curb near our house for half an hour just checking things out before I had to give up. That's 'cause there was nothing *to* check out. No kids playing in the street. No old people sitting on the front steps and talking to each other. No doors slamming as people came in and out of their houses. Because the garages were connected to the houses, I didn't even see anybody getting in or out of their cars. This neighborhood was nothing like Roxbury.

Fifth of all, it was too dark in this new room. How's a person supposed to sleep without the lamp on because her nerdy sister reads in bed until she falls asleep? I couldn't bother Aeisha anymore by hiding the light bulb from the lamp and taking the batteries out of her backup flashlight. I couldn't pretend to be asleep so I could see where she was hiding her diary that night. What was Aeisha gonna do without me to find her glasses in the morning, 'cause she's blind without them and she never remembers where she put them?

Sixth of all . . . I peeked up at the ceiling again.

Dad had got the stars all wrong. Ursa Minor was supposed to be over in the corner, with Orion right over my head. I couldn't even tell which constellation Dad had put up there. That wasn't like Dad. Hadn't he used the star chart that came with the box? Didn't he think I would be able to tell the difference?

I figured I had six good reasons to get out of bed now, so I did.

I walked slowly to the door and opened it a crack. I could see lights under Khatib's and Aeisha's doors, and I could hear the water running downstairs, so I knew that Mama and Dad were still downstairs unpacking. I walked to the top of the stairs and sat down.

Mama sure could hold a grudge. She hadn't even come to my room to wish me good night. Maybe she was right. Maybe everybody would miss the old neighborhood as much as I would. And maybe Aeisha was right, too. Maybe I *had* been a little bit of a brat all week. Mama and Dad didn't even know about Operation Obstruction of Justice, but they didn't like my attitude.

And nothing had gone right that day, either. The moving truck got lost and didn't find our house until after dark. We got a flat tire right after we left the house and we had to unload the whole car in the middle of a parking lot so Dad could get to the spare tire, which turned out to be flat, too.

When we finally got to the new house, our neighbors just stared at us through the windows. I must have said "I told you so" a million times, and I guess it was one too many times, 'cause Mama blew up at me.

"Tell me why you think you're the only person in this family with feelings, Ola," Mama snapped when I complained about how high the kitchen cabinets were. "You think none of us is sad to be leaving the old neighborhood, too? Well, we are. But here we are all trying to make the best of it, and so busy trying to keep you happy that we can't show our own sadness. Watch out, Ola, because you are working my last good nerve."

Now, sitting in the dark at the top of the stairs, I listened to the clinking noises she was making as she unpacked the plates downstairs. I knew I wouldn't be able to go to sleep until I made up with her.

"Ola, what are you doing?" Khatib's voice made me jump. He was standing behind me in his blue pajamas. Half of his face was shadowed, making him look scary.

"I'm contemplating," I whispered, using one of Aeisha's words.

I heard a giggle. Aeisha was standing behind Khatib.

"Contemplating what?" Aeisha asked, moving down to sit on the stair below me. She had on her favorite red bathrobe. "Your atrocious behavior? Your insensitivity? The fact that Mama had to—"

"Thanks, Aeisha," I cut her off. "I feel bad enough already."

Khatib sat down beside me and stretched his legs. They were so long they stretched down five steps, while mine only stretched past two and a half. One good thing about this move was that it had made Khatib spend more time with the family. I would never admit it to him, but I'd missed having him around since he started high school. "Just apologize, Ola," he said.

I nodded and stared into the carpet. It was light green and thick. Aeisha wouldn't have to worry about getting her feet dirty. Another change. I missed our old house so bad it hurt.

"So what do you think?" Aeisha whispered. She started playing with the belt of her bathrobe.

"Think about what?"

Aeisha pushed her glasses up her nose and squinted at us intently. "About the neighborhood . . . you know."

"Know what?" I asked.

Khatib was nodding like he knew what Aeisha was talking about.

"It looks boring," I said. "And this whole cooperative thing sounds stupid. Some kid across the street left his bike outside again, and I checked from my window twice and it's still there. I guess you don't have to worry about thieves here—"

"No welcome committee," Aeisha interrupted me. Her brown eyes were serious.

"Huh?" I asked.

Aeisha sighed impatiently. "If it had been anybody else, there would have been a welcome committee. You know—somebody with a pie or a cake to welcome us into the neighborhood."

"Maybe they don't have a welcome committee," I

suggested. I had been right about this place being unfriendly.

"Places like this always have a welcome committee," Aeisha said. "Don't you watch TV?"

"Maybe they don't come on Saturdays." I shrugged.

"It's 'cause we're black, Ola," Khatib said, elbowing me. He had his usual bored-with-the-world look on his face, but this time I could tell he was faking it.

"Oh, that," I said, leaning my head on my hands and feeling depressed. Number two on my list. The thing I didn't want to think about. We'd been in the new house for over ten hours already and made two trips to the supermarket, one to the hardware store and another to a restaurant for dinner. And everyplace we went, people stared at us. It felt weird not seeing any other black people—anywhere. Just us. It was one thing to know that before we moved in, but it was another thing to actually experience it. "Maybe the welcome committee will come tomorrow."

"Maybe it won't," said Aeisha.

"Doesn't matter if it does or doesn't." Dad's voice came from the bottom of the stairs, making Khatib, Aeisha and me look down. Dad was standing behind Mama with his hands on her shoulders. Grady was standing behind them, looking up at all of us, too. Dad had gone to pick him up from the pound that afternoon.

"Is this a Benson kids' meeting, or can any Benson join?"

Khatib and Aeisha rolled their eyes. Dad sounded so lame. We'd had three meetings that week already (most of which I'd boycotted). Dad was very big on sitting us all down to discuss our concerns as a family unit.

"Any Benson can join," I said cheerfully. Maybe what we needed was a family meeting. After all, Khatib, Aeisha and I had some serious concerns here. Maybe discussing it as a family unit would help. Best of all, maybe Mama would see that I was trying to cooperate and stop being mad at me. I looked at her hopefully.

"Glad to see you're participating, Ola." Mama arched one of her long eyebrows and looked back at me. It wasn't going to be that easy. Mama can be a tough nut to crack, boy.

Grady climbed up the stairs and nuzzled me with his nose before going to sit between Aeisha and Khatib. So far, he was the only good thing about this move.

"First order of business?" Dad asked, after he and Mama had settled on the stairs below us.

"We really are the *only* black people in this neighborhood?" Aeisha always gets right to the point.

"Yes."

Khatib and Aeisha were quiet for a few seconds, and I moved down one step.

"And we're really gonna be the *only* black people at our schools?"

"Yes."

I moved down another step. We were all quiet now, and I knew what everybody was thinking. Living in Boston, you know that there are rules. Everybody lives in their own neighborhoods. Everybody goes to their own schools. People break those rules all the time, but if they do, they usually end up on the six o'clock news. Were we gonna get in any trouble for living here? I moved down another step until I was squeezed in tight between Dad and Mama.

"So we're the *only* black people in this town?" Khatib asked slowly. "How are people gonna feel about us?"

"Everyone was staring at us all day," I muttered. Now that we were talking about it, I realized how much that had bothered me.

"How did you kids feel about the white students in your old school?" Dad asked quietly.

I hadn't thought about that before. Our old school was mostly black and Hispanic, but there were a few white kids who went there, too. It was true that they stood out, but after a while you got used to them. Most of them lived in the same neighborhoods as the rest of us, anyway, and they acted just like us. But *we* didn't come from here. I didn't know how to explain it to Dad, but this was different, and I knew that Khatib and Aeisha felt the same way.

"How are they supposed to feel about us?" Dad asked, changing the question.

"Well, we came from a bad neighborhood," Khatib said, frowning. He was plucking at strands in the carpet nervously. "The news calls it a bad neighborhood, anyway."

"We came from a community," Mama corrected huffily. All of us looked at her with relief. Dad usually does the talking when there's really something to worry about and he wants to prepare us for it — like when Aunt Josephine, Uncle Louis's wife, died last year from cancer or when he and Mama both had to work on Christmas last year and we had to spend Christmas day with old Aunt Mary. But when Mama does the talking, it means nothing is gettin' in our way, 'cause she won't let it, and Mama *always* has her way. "And this is a community, too. Might be a different one, but all that means is that it'll take time for us to adjust to it. You were right, Ola. There is no welcome committee. But you were right, too, Aeisha. It's strange and shameful that none of these neighbors has come by to say hello. Guess it'll take time for them to adjust to us, too. You'll see. Soon people will stop staring and we won't be such a novelty."

I leaned my head against Mama's arm. "I'm sorry I've been a pain."

Mama put her arm around me. "You all have school tomorrow. I want everybody in bed soon."

Khatib, Aeisha and I nodded, but none of us moved. Somehow the thought of a new school where we didn't know anybody was worse than moving into this new house. At least here we had each other. I noticed Khatib was frowning, and I wondered if he was worried about his tryout for the basketball team the next day. Aeisha didn't have too much to worry about. She was being placed in an advanced sixth-grade class that had a bunch of other brainy kids, so she would fit right in. But what about me? I didn't have a team or a class to fit into. What if no one wanted to be friends with me? What if this school and this neighborhood couldn't handle someone as unusual as me?

"Did you hear that?" Khatib asked. His eyes were wide.

"What?" I asked. Mama, Dad and Aeisha were sitting very still. Grady had his head perked. "Did the faucet explode?" Mama had tried to fix a leaky faucet in the kitchen that afternoon, and there's always trouble whenever Mama tries to fix anything. One time she tried to change the oil in the car and Dad ended up having to rebuild practically the whole engine.

"Shhh, Ola. Listen." Aeisha kicked my shoulder with her foot.

"Hey—" I started to turn around and yell at Aeisha when I heard a faint knocking sound coming from downstairs. It was so soft, I could barely hear it. Then Grady started barking.

"What now?" Mama sighed, standing up and starting down the stairs. Dad followed her. "Quiet, Grady."

"Someone's at the door," Aeisha whispered, standing up to look over the railing. She had her hand on Grady's collar.

"We don't know anybody here," Khatib said, leaning over to peer through the balusters.

"Maybe it's the neighbors." I stood up and leaned over the banister, too.

"Maybe it's some maniac," Aeisha whispered.

Mama and Dad were looking through the peephole.

"Maybe somebody stole that kid's bike and he wants to know if we saw anything," I said, trying not to show how nervous I was. "If he thinks we did it, you should kick his butt, Khatib."

"No way. These hands are my secret weapons for tomorrow." Khatib nudged me with his elbow. "Why don't *you* kick his butt?"

I didn't answer 'cause just then Dad opened the door and a tall girl wearing the strangest clothes walked in and kissed Dad right on the cheek.

"Lillian," Aeisha guessed first, and Khatib and I nodded. We all remembered from Marie-Thérèse's house that Haitians kiss each other hello and goodbye on the cheek. Sure enough, the tall girl kissed Mama's cheek too, then just stood looking down at the floor. Mama started talking to her, but she was speaking so softly we couldn't hear what she was saying.

"What's she wearing?" Khatib whispered, trying not to laugh.

"Clothes." Aeisha frowned at Khatib.

I didn't say anything. We couldn't see the girl's face very well from the top of the stairs, but we could see her bunchy yellow turtleneck that was too short in the arms and her long purple and black flowered skirt that was too big. She also had on knee-high gray sweat socks, like Khatib wears for basketball practice, and black patent leather shoes with the strap across the middle, like the ones little girls wear. The only thing she had with her was a crumpled brown paper bag, which she was holding tight against her stomach.

Mama turned around and motioned all of us to come down. "Come and say hello to Lillian before you go to bed."

I headed down first 'cause I wanted to get a good look at this person who would be living with us and especially taking care of *me* after school. It would be hard for anybody to live up to Mrs. Gransby, and I intended to let Mama and Dad and this new girl know that. As I walked down the hallway I looked at her more closely. Everything about this girl was tall and bony. She had long, bony arms and legs, and a long, skinny neck. Her skin was deep reddish brown, and her hair was curled in tight rolls around her head. I couldn't see her face very well 'cause she still had her head bowed.

Dad put his hands on my shoulders and pushed me forward. "Lillian, this is Ayeola, the youngest."

"Just Ola," I said. I heard her whisper *"Bonswa,"* but she didn't lift her head.

"Hi," I said, before Dad pulled me away and nodded for Khatib to come up. It's hard to size up somebody who won't look at you. Lillian whispered the same thing to them, and I wondered what it meant, but from the look Mama was giving me I could tell she was telling me not to bother Lillian that night. As soon as Aeisha finished introducing herself, Mama looked at the three of us and said, "Bed."

We nodded and turned around to go up the stairs. I looked back to see if Lillian was watching us, but she had her eyes on the floor. I started to think about how strange it must be to leave your country and come someplace new, and I realized that we had something in common with Lillian. All of us had moved to a new place, and none of us had any idea what to expect. At least me and Khatib and Aeisha had Mama and Dad, though. Lillian had left everybody she knew behind in another country.

Chapter Four

Ola the Gangster

When I came downstairs for breakfast the next morning, Lillian wasn't there. Dad said she needed her rest and that we would have time to get to know her later, but I was disappointed. I wanted to know more about her and why she wore such strange clothes.

"What time does the school bus come?" I asked, climbing up on one of the stools. Mama had gone all out for our first day of school. There were eggs, bacon, grits and toast piled up on our plates.

"Your dad's going to drive you to school," Mama said. She touched my shoulder as she passed behind me to the other side of the counter.

"How come?" Aeisha asked. She was slathering three pieces of toast with margarine.

"Just for this first day," Mama said. She sat down on one of the stools and ate a big spoonful of grits without saying anything else.

I pushed the food around my plate with my fork. Mama

hadn't answered the question, but I knew they thought it would be easier on us if they drove us to school. I didn't feel much like eating.

Mama looked at me and sighed. "Ola—"

Before she could say anything else, Grady started barking and ran out of the kitchen. In between his barks, we could hear someone knocking at the front door. Again.

"What *now*?" Mama asked, standing up. "When it rains, it pours around here."

Aeisha and I followed Mama to the door. We'd only been in the house one day and we'd already had two visitors. Mama looked through the peephole and frowned. She looked back at us. "It's a woman standing in her bathrobe."

"Her bathrobe?" I repeated. Two visitors and both of them dressed wrong.

Mama opened the door, and Aeisha and I peeked around her. A woman about Mama's age was standing on our front steps in a blue terry-cloth bathrobe. The lady was white, with long blond hair straggling around her face. Her face was long and thin and she had dark circles under her eyes. She looked like she had just gotten out of bed.

"Welcome to the neighborhood." The woman pushed out her hands. She was holding a homemade pie. "It's pumpkin. Made from Walcott's world-famous pumpkins. I tried to get over yesterday, but the baby cried so."

Mama took the pie. "Well, thank you, Mrs. . . ?"

"Adele. Adele Spunklemeyer, from across the street." The woman blinked tiredly.

"We're very grateful, Mrs. Spunklemeyer." Mama smiled

kindly at the woman. "I'm Fatima Benson and these are my daughters, Aeisha and Ayeola."

"I would have made a cake, but I was afraid the baby's crying would make it fall." Mrs. Spunklemeyer sighed and looked very sorry.

"I know how much work new babies can be." Mama nodded in sympathy.

"He's not new. He's eight months old, but he cries so." Mrs. Spunklemeyer gazed at me and Aeisha and sighed again. "Girls. Maybe if I'd had a girl, she wouldn't cry so."

Aeisha and I looked at each other and tried not to laugh. All Mrs. Spunklemeyer could talk about was her crying baby.

"Sorry to come over in my robe and all, but he cries so." Mrs. Spunklemeyer turned around. "Goodbye. I must get back."

"Goodbye," Mama called out after her. We watched as Mrs. Spunklemeyer shuffled back across the street and into her house. As she opened the door, we could hear the sound of a baby wailing from somewhere inside. "That poor woman."

"*She's* our Welcome Wagon?" Aeisha said, raising her eyebrows. She started laughing, and Mama and I joined her. Mrs. Spunklemeyer was going to be a funny neighbor.

We told Dad and Khatib about Mrs. Spunklemeyer when they came down for breakfast, and they laughed, too. It made all of us feel better about the day ahead — for a little while. While Dad was driving us to school, Khatib, Aeisha and I stared out the window. Our dead neighborhood had been transformed. Kids ran out of their houses or walked along the street, and parents were getting into their cars to drive to work. There were old lady crossing guards everywhere. Dad was frustrated because he couldn't drive more than fifteen miles an hour in a school zone. When we pulled up in front of the high school, Khatib jumped out of the car without even saying goodbye or looking back. Soon we couldn't see the back of his blue jacket as he blended into the other students entering the building. The high school was huge. It had three long brick buildings that stretched around the block, and WALCOTT HIGH SCHOOL was spelled out in blue and yellow paint on the walkway. Aeisha and I looked at each other, thinking the same thing. Our old school had been big, but not *this* big. If our school was as big as Khatib's, we'd never find our way to our classrooms.

When Dad finally pulled up in front of a square stone building, I sighed with relief. It looked bigger than our old school, but at least it was only one building. It looked really old, too. There was ivy growing from cracks all over the front, and the stones it was made of looked smooth and worn.

"Built in 1883," Dad chirped.

Aeisha and I ignored him. Dad and Mama had been killing us with little facts about historic Walcott all week. I don't know why they thought it would impress us that Walcott was as old as the Pilgrims. That was one of the things I found strange about our neighborhood. The rest of Walcott was old. In downtown Walcott, all the streets were made of cobblestones and the houses were built in that old style that Dad said was called "colonial." Our neighborhood, with its brand-new look-alike houses, didn't seem to fit into this town at all. Just like us.

There were three big yellow school buses lined up in front of the school, and kids were pouring out of them. Aeisha and I sat there for a while and watched them without saying anything.

"The schoolyard is in the back," Dad said, clearing his throat and looking at us. "They also have a track, a football field and a swimming pool."

"Great," Aeisha answered halfheartedly. Our old school had no track, no football field and no swimming pool — which explained why most of our sports teams never won anything. But Aeisha and I could walk to our old school instead of taking a dumb bus, and if we'd still been at our old school, Aeisha would already have been in the cafeteria tutoring and I would have been in the schoolyard playing Chinese jump rope with Karen and Margarita.

Dad looked at his watch and back at us. It was his first day of work. Before we'd left Roxbury, he'd gone and got another haircut. I was glad he was starting work before he went completely bald. "You want me to walk in with you?"

"No way," I said, grabbing my backpack. "Come on, Aeisha."

Aeisha followed me out of the car, and then we both stood there and looked at Dad. We'd both tried to dress normal so we could blend in. Aeisha had on jeans and a green polo shirt underneath her winter jacket, and I had on a blue T-shirt and brown corduroy overalls. The only thing that stood out on us was our shiny and unmarked new sneakers, which were a must for any first day at school.

Dad looked at us and nodded. "Oka
"Okay." I turned around. "Come o,
We tried to walk toward the frc
slowly, but the other kids pushed us
us I could feel people staring at u.
nore them. Then I heard some tall boy w...
"Move along, stupid new kids," but before I couu
around to ask him who he was calling stupid, he was gone
and we were inside the building. Aeisha and I stood in the
middle of a hallway that had a marble floor with black and
white squares on it. I could tell people were still staring at
us because that hot prickly feeling that I had felt in the
restaurant the day before was back.

"Kind of like being a movie star," Aeisha said, nodding to
herself. She looked at the piece of paper she had in her hand.
"You're on the second floor and I'm down this hallway."

"I know that." Dad had gone over our schedules with us
that morning.

"You want me to—"

"No way," I said, cutting her off. Why was everybody
treating me like I was a baby? "I'll see you after school."

"Okay. Meet me right here. We have to take the number
eight-oh-eight school bus and—"

"Yeah, yeah. See you later, Aeisha." I turned around and
joined the crowd headed up the stairs in the middle of the
hallway. This time I moved as fast as everyone else so no one
would say anything. I knew from my schedule that my
homeroom was number 213 and that the teacher's name was
Mrs. Woodstein. When I got to the classroom, I saw a girl
with long, flat brown hair leaning against the wall beside the

he only reason I noticed her at all was because the
ad attitude. She had on tight jeans and a colorful tie-
d T-shirt, and she was slouching against the wall like it
as her wall and she belonged there. I expected her to take
out a cigarette at any minute and blow a puff of smoke in the
air, just like the tough kids at my old school, who always
hung out behind the building or in the second-floor bathroom. The other thing that made me notice this girl was that
she didn't stare at me. She just looked at me and looked
away like I was nobody special.

"That's Maria Poncinelli," I heard someone say from behind me. I looked and saw another girl with blue eyes and
the frizziest brown hair I had ever seen.

"What's her problem?" I asked.

"She's the mayor's daughter," the girl said, disappearing
into the classroom before I could ask her what that meant.
I looked back at the girl against the wall. Maria Poncinelli
didn't look like a mayor's daughter. I couldn't imagine her
being a model citizen.

I was kind of glad to see there was somebody at this
school like Maria Poncinelli. It gave me hope that this
school just might be able to accept someone as unusual as
me. Unfortunately, that hope faded as soon as I walked into
the classroom. Everybody stopped talking and laughing and
stared at me as I walked over to Mrs. Woodstein's desk. I
wished I'd got lost trying to find the classroom. I wished I'd
stayed outside with Maria Poncinelli. I even wished I'd let
Dad or Aeisha walk me to homeroom. Most of all, I wished
I was back at my old school in my old neighborhood, where
I could know that people were staring at me because I was

the new kid and not because of anything else. Back at my old school, having everyone's full attention like this would have been the opportunity of a lifetime to do something or say something funny, but here I didn't think anybody would laugh at anything I had to say.

I stopped in front of Mrs. Woodstein's desk and handed her my schedule. I could tell she was a new teacher because she was pretty young and she didn't have either that tired, worn-out look or that hard-nosed, don't-mess-with-me look that experienced teachers have. She had long blond hair and she was wearing light blue eye shadow and a pink flowered dress. She was also smiling so hard it made me nervous.

"Welcome, Ayeola," she said, not even looking at my schedule, and pronouncing my name exactly right. Impressive.

"Just Ola," I corrected, nodding.

Mrs. Woodstein stood up, still smiling. "Class, this is our new student, Ola Benson. Say hello."

Half the class said hi and the other half just continued looking. I wanted to stare at the floor, but I forced myself to look back. There's nothing worse than a new kid who looks scared.

"Ola comes to us from . . . ?" Mrs. Woodstein waited for me to fill in the answer.

"Roxbury," I muttered at first, then I straightened up. I was proud of where I came from. "In Boston."

No one said anything. I noticed that the classroom was bigger than my old homeroom, but there were only half as many kids. Dad had boasted that one of the best things about the Walcott school system was that there was more individual attention. From a parent's point of view, I guess that's important, but for students it means it's easier for the teacher to keep an eye on what you're doing. It means you get picked more often to answer the homework questions. It means no sneaking off to the rest room for a long time with three of your friends without the teacher noticing. There couldn't have been more than twenty kids in the classroom. Now, I'm not a juvenile delinquent. I do all my homework and get decent grades. I even pay attention to the lessons most of the time. But school can get pretty boring, and you need something to shake it up every once in a while. I was always a shake-things-up kind of student. Things like letting the class pet out of its cage and putting signs on people's backs were my specialty. Harmless and anonymous stuff. But with only twenty people to a classroom, it was gonna be awfully hard to be anonymous. Being the only black kid in the class was gonna make it impossible. Suddenly, looking out at all those other students, I realized that my school pest career was probably over. I was gonna have to become like Aeisha and get perfect grades and be an upstanding student. I felt depressed.

"Ola." Mrs. Woodstein, who was standing next to me, put one hand on my shoulder softly. "Every new student has a buddy for their first day."

"A buddy?"

"Someone who gives you a tour of the school, makes sure that you get to all your classes okay and introduces you to people that you should know." Mrs. Woodstein was still smiling. "Someone has already volunteered to be your buddy."

I wanted to say, "Oh, yeah?" in a really tough way, but I didn't. This buddy system seemed kind of fishy to me. In my old school, anybody who would volunteer for such a position was someone you didn't want to be friends with—either the class bully or the class pet, or sometimes the class weirdo.

"Anna, come up and introduce yourself to Ola." To my relief, Mrs. Woodstein turned her smile away from me to someone else in the classroom. In the third row, a girl with a blond ponytail stood up and started walking toward me. I had her sized up within three seconds. Class pet—type A. Anna was a short, dumpy girl with a moon face, gray eyes, and a nose that turned up like a pig's. She was wearing a blue dress like the kind Mama would point out in the store for me when she's joking because she knows I'd say, "No way—too babyish." Anna definitely looked like the type of person I would not get along with.

When she finally reached the front of the class, she held out her hand and gave me a phony smile. "Anna Banaster."

"Hi," I said. Up close, Anna seemed more like the class snob than the class pet. She had on a gold necklace and a bracelet, both with her name spelled on them. At my old school, you learned fast not to wear gold around where everybody could see it—it would get stolen easy. I figured this was like that kid who left his bike on the lawn all night. I'd checked first thing that morning and the bike was still there. The kid was practically *giving* it away, but no one cared. And from the way Anna was looking at me, I could tell she was sizing me up. I wondered why she had volunteered to show me around. "Just call me Ola."

"Okay, Ola." Anna had barely touched my hand when the bell for first period rang, and she dropped it like a hot potato. "Come on, I'll get you to your first class."

I followed Anna. I felt relieved I'd gotten through home-room.

As we stepped out the door we were joined by two of Anna's friends, Daphne and Diane. They were twins, and both had long brown hair that went all the way down to the middle of their backs. They weren't wearing dresses, but, like Anna, they had necklaces and bracelets with their names on them, too. It was like they were part of some se-cret club and Anna Banaster was the president. Daphne and Diane did everything Anna told them to do.

"She's gotta go to history, room B-six," Anna ordered, passing me off. "I'll pick her up after that."

Then Anna just walked away. The last thing I noticed be-fore following Daphne and Diane was Maria Poncinelli, still leaning against the wall outside of homeroom but with a big smirk on her face.

Daphne and Diane didn't say anything to me, but every once in a while one of them would glance at me real fast, then look away. It didn't take me long to figure out that they were scared of me. When I moved my hand to hitch my school bag higher, both of them moved a little further away. Normally I would think that this was very funny, but this time I didn't. I hadn't given them *any* reason to be scared of me — not yet, anyway. Normally this would be a good situa-tion to take advantage of, but for some reason I felt like I needed to put them at ease and show them that I was a reg-ular person, just like them.

"Hi," I said experimentally.

Daphne and Diane looked at each other before answer-ing me. Finally they mumbled hi in my direction while moving an inch further away from me. That really bothered me. When we reached room B-6 I went inside without saying anything to them, and I made sure I was out of the classroom before Anna Banaster could show up to take me to my next class. I wasn't going to waste any more of my time making people I didn't even like feel better about me.

The rest of the day went just as bad until lunch. Most people didn't seem to care about me one way or the other, but there were a few who kept staring at me. Nobody except the teachers said much of anything to me. In the schoolyard, I went looking for Aeisha to see if the same thing was happening to her, but I couldn't find her. Finally I sat down at a bench in a corner of the schoolyard. I remembered what Mama had said about people needing time to adjust to us, and I wondered how long that was going to take. This whole move had been one big mistake.

"Hey."

I looked up to find the girl with the frizzy hair from my homeroom standing next to me. She was wearing a huge red-and-white striped poncho with big side pockets.

"What'd you do with them?" she asked, sticking her hands into the pockets.

"With who?"

The girl rolled her eyes. "You know—Anna Banana and the ding-dong girls."

I shrugged.

The girl sat down beside me. "It's kind of hard to get rid of Anna."

"Not if you're me," I said seriously. I'd seen Anna Banaster twice since homeroom and both times she'd kept her distance. Just like everybody else at this school, I thought.

"Well, who're you?"

I looked at her, surprised. "I'm just Ola."

The girl looked me up and down. "Well, that doesn't sound too scary to *me*."

I stared at her. This girl was strange. For a second I wondered if I had finally run into the class weirdo.

"So what's it like?"

"What's what like?"

"Roxbury. Everybody says you moved here because it was too dangerous there. Gangs and shootings and everything."

"My neighborhood was a good one. Just because we don't have huge houses and schools with swimming pools doesn't mean good people don't live there," I said hotly.

The girl shrugged. "So okay. Sorry."

"We moved here 'cause of my parents' jobs," I said loudly. "Anything wrong with that?"

The girl shook her head and was quiet for a moment. Then she stood up. "Well, I better be moseying along now. I have to patrol the schoolyard."

I stared at her, annoyed but almost sorry she was leaving. As stupid as her questions had been, at least she had clued me in to what was going on with Daphne and Diane and all the stares Aeisha and I had been getting. It wasn't just 'cause we were black or the new kids here. The whole school probably thought Aeisha and I were gangsters. I tried to picture me looking tough in a black bomber jacket and carrying a switchblade. Ola the gangster? I was only nine years old! Then I tried to picture Aeisha in the same outfit and had to laugh out loud.

When the bell rang to go back to class, I finally saw Aeisha across the schoolyard, and she didn't look too good either. She was sitting on one of the benches on the other side of the schoolyard, hunkered over one of her textbooks. I could tell from the way her shoulders were hunched that she was worried about something. I wondered if she'd found out what everybody in this school thought about us. Then I noticed something strange. There was a short boy sitting at the other end of the bench, watching her. When she got up to go inside, he stood up and followed right behind her. I hurried to keep up with them and watched as he followed Aeisha all the way up to the third floor and into the same classroom, always staying right behind her. Once I saw Aeisha look back at him, but she didn't seem too upset. Who was he? What did he want with my sister? As soon as I saw Aeisha after school I was going to find out.

The rest of the day went pretty much like the morning. In my math class I found out that the name of the girl who'd talked to me in the schoolyard was River, but she didn't say anything to me or even look at me in class. I also had three classes with Maria Poncinelli, who was leaning against the wall outside before and after each one. Most of the teachers sent someone outside to drag her in when they started their lessons. By the time I went to meet Aeisha in the front hallway after school, I was ready to go home — or back to our new house, anyway.

Aeisha was waiting for me just where she'd said she would. She had a mountain of books in her arms and she still looked worried. I looked around, and sure enough, the short boy was standing not too far behind her, watching her. I put on one of my meanest looks, ready to scare him off. But then I got a really good look at him.

"Who's that?" I asked Aeisha.

Aeisha glanced back and shrugged. "That's Otis. He's in my advanced science class."

I looked again and tried to keep from laughing. Otis looked like he was falling apart. His shoelaces were untied, half of his shirt was hanging out of his jeans and he'd missed almost all the loops for his belt. That wasn't all, either. Otis had short brown-blond hair that stuck out all over his head like a porcupine's quills and his glasses were sitting crooked on his face. His blue school bag had a big hole in it. He'd left a trail of pencils and papers down the hallway. Behind his glasses I could see that Otis was a little cross-eyed. And both of his crossed eyes were stuck on Aeisha.

"What does he want?" I asked Aeisha in a whisper.

"I don't know. All I did was take a sign off his back," Aeisha muttered, starting to walk to the front door. "Come on. Bus number eight-oh-eight."

"What happened?" I asked Aeisha as soon as we sat down on the bus. I noticed that Otis was sitting in the seat behind us. I wondered if he was still following Aeisha or if he belonged on this bus. It was just like Aeisha to take that sign off his back. She doesn't like it when people make fun of other people. But something else was bothering her.

"So how was it?" I asked when Aeisha didn't answer me the first time. I wanted to see if she felt the same way I had all day — like we were onstage acting, with the whole school for our audience. I wanted to know if she thought the same way I did about the colors being different here. I couldn't get used to seeing so many blue-, green- or gray-eyed people, and hardly any of the girls had short hair. None of them wore braids like me. But most of all I wanted to get Aeisha's opinion on this whole gangster thing and see if it bothered her as much as it bothered me.

Aeisha shrugged and looked out the window. She wouldn't say anything else the whole way home. She must have had a really bad day, too, 'cause she didn't even read her romance novel on the way, though I knew she had packed one that morning. She just flipped through the pages of her new books. None of the other kids on the bus said anything to us, but a few of them stared. When we got off the bus, I heard somebody say, "Bye, black girls," and start laughing, but when I turned around, I couldn't tell who it was. Aeisha pulled me off the bus without saying anything and started walking fast to our house. I walked more slowly because, first, I wanted to see if Aeisha could even find our house, and second, I was watching Otis. He'd gotten off the bus with us and was trying to keep up with Aeisha — which wasn't easy to do with his shoelaces untied. A couple of times I thought he was going to crash on the sidewalk and break his head.

"Who's that?" I heard Aeisha ask ahead of me.

I turned to see what she was talking about and noticed an old lady and an old man staring at us from the windows of their house. They both had gray hair and pink, wrinkled skin, and both of them were frowning at us.

"Mr. and Mrs. Stern," I heard Otis say. It was the first

time I'd heard him speak, and I was surprised that he didn't have a high, squeaky voice to go with his appearance. His voice sounded normal. "They watch everybody."

"How come?" I asked, catching up with them.

"They're in charge of the neighborhood association," Otis said, as if that explained everything.

I looked back at them one more time. They didn't look very friendly.

Aeisha found our house with no problem. She didn't even have to look at the number. When we all got to the front door, she pulled me inside and turned around to say, "Go home, Otis," before shutting the door in his face.

I dropped my school bag, patted Grady, who was sitting at the bottom of the stairs, and went straight to the big window in the living room to see if Otis had listened to her. Sure enough, Otis was walking away from our house slowly. When he got to the sidewalk, he turned around to look back, as if to see whether Aeisha was really gone. Then he crossed the street and walked right into the house across from us. The same one Mrs. Spunklemeyer had gone into.

Otis was one of our neighbors.

"Aeisha!" I shouted, turning around. I didn't see Aeisha anywhere, but her new sneakers were sitting at the bottom of the stairs. "The kid across the street who left his bike outside is Otis! Can you believe it? He's a Spunklemeyer! Aeisha!"

"Ola, *what* are you screaming for?" I looked, and there was Mama sticking her head out from behind the kitchen door. Boy, was I glad to see her.

"Aeisha's got a boyfriend and he lives right across the

street. He must be one of Mrs. Spunklemeyer's kids," I said, coming into the kitchen and giving her a tight hug. "And something's bothering Aeisha, but she won't tell what it is. When do we get out of here?" I'd given this neighborhood and this school a chance and it hadn't worked.

Mama cocked her head to one side and rolled her eyes. "Do you ever give up?" Her hair was pulled back into a big, bushy ponytail and she was wearing jeans and a T-shirt, 'cause she'd spent the day unpacking.

"Mama—" I was about to explain my whole day at school when I noticed who else was in the kitchen. With all this school stuff, I'd forgotten about Lillian. She was unpacking pots and pans and putting them in one of the cabinets. She had on an ugly green-and-white polka-dot dress that looked like it used to be somebody's party dress, and gray sweat socks pulled up to her knees. I wondered who'd given her all those strange clothes.

Khatib was in the kitchen, too, perched on one of the stools, and I could tell that he was trying not to laugh every time he looked at Lillian. Then I noticed that Khatib had a big plate of rice and peas sitting right in front of him.

"Hey, Ola," Khatib said in between mouthfuls.

I walked over to look at his food and sniffed. It smelled a lot like Mrs. Gransby's food. "Where'd you get that?"

"Lillian made it," Mama said, smiling at Lillian.

I looked over at Lillian and saw that she was opening and closing one cabinet door. She did it several times, like she was trying to figure out how it worked. Then she stuck her head inside the cabinet to look at the latch. Weird. I thought it was kind of unfair that she got to spend the whole day with

Mama by herself while I had to go to school. But on the other hand, if she could make rice and peas like Mrs. Gransby, then maybe she was worth keeping. I walked over to stand by her and said, "Hi, Lillian," in a really loud voice.

Lillian looked down, surprised, and I got my first look at her eyes. They were cat-shaped and a dark molasses color. They were beautiful, but they also were very sad.

I turned away and walked back to Mama. I needed another hug but I didn't want to look like a baby in front of Khatib. Mama was reading something on a piece of paper and not paying any attention to me.

"What's that?" I asked, leaning against her.

"It's the rules for the development. Mr. Stern from the neighborhood association dropped them off." Mama was frowning deeply. I wasn't surprised. Anything Mr. and Mrs. Stern dropped off couldn't be good. I leaned in to look at the paper, too, and my mouth dropped open. The list was a page long and had fifteen rules typed out in bold black letters. Right at the top was the one I already knew, about not hanging your clothes out in the yard, but there were a bunch of crazy rules, too, like not having visitors after 10 P.M., not having parties without informing the neighborhood association, and no playing outside except in the backyard. The worst one was the curfew for kids. No kids under sixteen could be outside after dark. There was also a whole bunch of recommendations on how often to cut your grass and what kind of flowers to plant in the spring.

I sniffed. "We have to follow all these rules?"

"It's for the good of the neighborhood. Keep it a safe place." Mama sighed. "It won't kill us to follow a few rules."

"So we can't play in the street and I can't go outside after seven o'clock?" I asked. Mama and Dad wouldn't let me go out after dark anyway, but that was a family rule, not a neighborhood rule. Whose business was it if Mama and Dad did let me stay out late or we hung a clothesline in our own backyard or we wanted to plant purple petunias instead of dogwoods?

Mama put the paper away and got up to take a plate out of one of the cabinets. "How was school?"

I climbed up on the stool opposite Khatib. I'd almost forgotten about how awful school had been. I started complaining right away. "They stuck me with Anna Banana and the ding-dong girls and nobody except this girl River talked to me."

"That's nothing. They're making me take a modern-dance class," Khatib muttered between mouthfuls of rice. "For PE. I have to wear tights."

I dug into the plate of rice and peas that Mama placed in front of me. "That's nothing. Everybody stared at me in homeroom, and the ding-dong girls acted like they were scared of me."

"That's nothin'." Khatib put his fork down. "After my try-out I heard one of the guys on the team say that I would make the team 'cause I'm black."

"Small potatoes," I said. "Some boy at school called us 'stupid new kids,' and then some other boy on the school bus said, 'Bye, black girls,' when we got off the bus. And this girl River said everyone thinks we came here because our old neighborhood was too dangerous. The whole school probably thinks we're gangsters."

Mama sat down on the stool next to me. She was frowning. "Are the two of you okay?"

Khatib and I looked at each other carefully. I was okay, I guessed. It didn't so much hurt me what people at school thought about me, but it did bother me a lot. I could tell Khatib felt the same way.

"Because you know that all that comes from just plain ignorance." Mama put her hands on my shoulders and squeezed gently. "When people get to know you for who you are, those perceptions will die down."

"What if they don't?" Khatib asked quietly.

"Then we'll deal with it." Mama nodded. She said it just as quietly as Khatib, but I knew that Mama's kind of quietness meant business. I started to feel a little better.

"Did anything *good* happen to you two today?" Mama picked up the list of rules and started frowning again.

Khatib and I looked at each other.

"I made the team." Khatib shrugged.

"The school has a swimming pool." I shrugged, too.

Both of us were quiet after that. Lillian had finished unpacking one of the boxes and went to the other side of the kitchen to get another one. She picked it up like it weighed nothing and carried it back.

Then I heard Mama sigh and say, "Well, it's a start."

But the start of what? So far it had been a horrible day, and worrying about what everybody thought about me at school had left me feeling restless. Watching Mama read the rules, I started to get an idea. Mama wasn't the only one around here who could take care of business.

Chapter Five

Operation Don't Get Stuck in Walcott

At four o'clock in the morning it was pretty dark outside.

I looked around our huge backyard and shivered. It was freezing. The wind was making a soft rustling sound as it blew through the trees, and my sneakers made a squishing noise as I walked across the wet grass. It was kind of scary out here in the dark. All the lights in the house were off, and the little bit of moon that was out made everything look shadowy. I was breaking two of the neighborhood rules by being out here, but I was gonna show this neighborhood that the Bensons didn't have to follow anybody's rules but their own. For now, this house was our house and what we did in it or around it was our own business.

I reached down to pat Grady, glad that I had thought to bring him along. It made me feel better that I wasn't out here all alone. I had given Grady careful instructions to let me know if he smelled anyone or anything.

I moved toward the right side of the yard, close to the

fence, which went all the way around the yard. Grady followed behind me. He sat down and watched while I pulled my old super-deluxe long jump rope and a black T-shirt out from under my jacket and tossed them on the grass. Grady stood up and went to sniff them, then looked at me with his ears perked. I could tell he wanted to know what was going on.

"I'm gonna hang up our new clothesline, Grady," I whispered. I wasn't sure why I was whispering, but it seemed appropriate.

Grady smiled. Or at least he looked like he was smiling. He stuck out his tongue and panted. I patted his head, but I couldn't feel his soft fur through my thick mittens.

I picked up one end of the jump rope and turned toward the huge maple tree that stood next to the tall brown fence. I had to hang the clothesline high enough so that the neighbors would see it, which wasn't going to be easy since the fence was way taller than me.

I started to climb up the tree slowly, thinking about what a good thing it was that I was the best jungle gym climber to come out of Roxbury. I had never really climbed a tree before, but it couldn't be much different. In the dark, it was hard finding spaces big enough to put my foot on, but I managed to feel around until I did. Below me I could hear Grady making soft whimpers. He was probably scared that I was going to fall down and break my neck, but he didn't know that, being the best jungle gym climber, I knew exactly how to fall so that I wouldn't get hurt.

Grady let out a yelp, and I looked down. He really was worried about me.

"I'm okay, Grady," I whispered loudly. He was going to wake somebody up and blow my whole plan.

As soon as I'd climbed high enough so I could see over the fence, I looked around for a big branch to tie one end of the jump rope to. I was surprised to see that there were some icicles on some of the branches. It was colder than I thought. Finally I found a big branch, and I swung one end of the jump rope around and knotted it. Now all I had to do was tie the other end to the fence a little ways over.

Grady growled.

Uh-oh.

I looked down, hoping it wasn't Mama or Dad.

"Well, hello there, young lady."

I froze, hugging the tree. The voice came out of nowhere.

"Now, now, don't take fright and crack your head fallin' outta that tree."

Slowly I turned my head. There was an old man looking up at me from the corner of the neighbor's yard. He had long straight white hair that reached his shoulders, and a baseball hat on his head. It was so dark I couldn't see the rest of his face.

"Haven't had us a tree-climbing accident since last summer. Believe it was young Rosemary fell outta that tree in the town center." The old man kept talking and looking up at me. "Cracked her head good enough for four stitches. Rosemary Atkinson. Family's been around here since the Civil War."

Great. Another person with a history lesson about Walcott. I looked carefully at the old man and saw that he was wearing nothing but his bathrobe, pajamas and bedroom slippers. He was gonna freeze.

"Mister, what are you doing out here?" I asked curiously. He was the first person I'd met in this neighborhood besides Otis.

"Nightwatching." The old man shook his head. "Always nightwatch this time of year."

"What are you watching?" I asked. Was he senile? Mr. Roland from our old neighborhood is senile. He still thinks he's a general in the army during World War II. He calls all of the neighborhood kids "private" and is always ordering everyone off the street because of incoming bombs.

But the old man looked at me like I was the one that was crazy. "I'm watching the night. Believe I said that already."

"You're our neighbor?" I asked. This neighborhood was getting weirder by the second. First Mrs. Spunklemeyer and Otis. Now this old man. They should rename this place WALCOTT CORNERS: WHERE THE STRANGE AND THE SENILE RESIDE.

"Moses Elijah." The old man bobbed his head. "And you would be . . . ?"

"Just Ola."

The old man stepped back a couple of feet and whistled. "Lotta ice on that tree, Just Ola."

"No — it's just Ola. Not Just Ola."

"Believe that's what I said." The old man was looking at me like I was crazy again. "Mind if I ask you what you're doing climbing trees before sunlight?"

"I'm hanging a clothesline." I didn't bother to make up

anything or explain why. Even if Mr. Elijah did tell someone about the clothesline, that was exactly what I wanted.

"Right smart idea," he mumbled. "Time was when every family in Walcott had a proper clothesline in the yard. Never did see one hanging from a tree, though."

"It's a special clothesline." I checked Grady and saw that he was sitting by the tree, still whimpering. "Grady's worried about me. I gotta go, Mr. Elijah."

"Well, Just Ola, I'll wait and see that you get down outta that tree all right, and then I'll be gettin' back to my night-watching." Mr. Elijah bobbed his head again.

I didn't bother to correct him about my name. I knew that senile people believe what they want. We never could convince Mr. Roland that we were kids instead of soldiers. I smiled as I looked for a place to put my foot. It had been Margarita's idea to turn the whole thing into a game. Every time Mr. Roland told us about an incoming bomb, all of us would start running like crazy. Some of us would fall and pretend we were wounded. When Mr. Roland said it was safe, he would order us to go back in and help the wounded back to camp. I stuck my foot into a hole in the middle of the tree and moved down a little. Thinking about Margarita made me remember my phone call to her that afternoon. She'd told me the "Martians" had moved into our house already but not to worry, 'cause she and Karen were looking for a bigger house right in Roxbury for us to move into, since we had a dog and Lillian now.

"Now, pay attention to what you're doing, Just Ola," I heard Mr. Elijah call.

"Don't worry, Mr. Elijah," I called back. I wasn't too far from the bottom now. "I'm the best jungle gym climber to come—"

The next thing I knew, I was pressed facedown in the cold, wet grass with Grady running around me in circles and barking like crazy.

"I was doing my usual nightwatching," Mr. Elijah chuckled, lifting his mug of hot chocolate and sipping from it, "when I thought I saw a bear cub climbing up that big old maple tree in your yard."

Mama and Dad were both frowning deeply as Mr. Elijah talked. I picked up the hand mirror and looked at my face again. Mama had brought it down for me and ordered me to look what I'd done to myself.

"Haven't seen a bear in Walcott proper since that circus accident in 1973, when all them animals ran loose around the town." Mr. Elijah's face creased into a smile.

I stared at my left cheek, which was all swollen up, and the long red scratch on the top of my forehead. At least it was only my face. The big winter coat, gloves and boots had protected the rest of me. Climbing trees and climbing jungle gyms were two whole different things.

"As I got up closer to the tree there, I realized it wasn't a bear at all. It was a Just Ola!"

While Mr. Elijah cracked up, I considered reminding Mama and Dad that they were breaking the neighborhood rule about no late-night visitors. Then I decided that the less I said, the better off I'd be. Mama and Dad were both giving me looks to kill. Mama had already spread ointment on my face and checked all my limbs to see that I hadn't broken anything. Once she and Dad realized that I was okay, they had started getting mad.

"Just what in the world were you doing?" Mama exploded.

"My jump rope got stuck in the tree," I explained quickly. I'd had plenty of time to think of something while Mr. Elijah told his story. I knew that if I told Mama that I was doing this all for her, she wouldn't believe me.

"And just why did four o'clock in the morning seem like the best time to go climbing for it?" Mama asked. She was giving me that same look Mr. Elijah had been giving me earlier, like I was crazy.

"W-Well, I couldn't sleep," I stammered, looking away from Mama to Dad. I was hoping he would hurry up and give me my punishment. It's always the same. Mama does all the yelling and Dad gives out the punishments.

"Normally four o'clock in the morning wouldn't be such a bad time to be climbing trees," Mr. Elijah cut in. "It was just the wrong time of year. Too much ice around in the wintertime."

I tried to smile at Mr. Elijah for helping me out, but my cheek hurt too much. "Yeah."

"Yeah nothing." Mama put her hands on her hips. She looked like a witch, with her hair all over her face and her long flannel nightgown going all the way down to her feet. "Do we have to watch you every minute of the night, too, Ola?"

Mama looked really frustrated. She stared at me for a full minute in complete silence. I knew she was trying to figure out what was really going on with me. Finally she sighed and said, "You have to try, Ola."

I looked away from her and nodded. From the corner of my eye, I saw Mama look at Dad and nod. Good — this was almost over.

"Dish duty every night this week. And straight home from school all month. No playing outside," Dad announced. He wiped his hand across his face like he was tired.

No playing outside? Had Dad forgotten where we lived? I didn't know anybody yet, and even if I did, there was a rule against playing outside on the street in this neighborhood.

"Okay," I said quickly, remembering how late Dad had come in from work the night before. Dad must have been really tired to let me get away so easy.

"We thank you, Mr. Elijah," Mama said, turning to where Mr. Elijah was sitting.

Mr. Elijah waved a hand in the air. "Not a problem. Glad to help a neighbor out these days. Don't get to do it much in this community, what with all the rules. People keep to themselves here."

Mama put her hands on the table. "So you haven't always lived here?"

"Family's been living in Walcott since 1812. Back then Walcott was a big mill town, and lots of folk were moving here for the work. My great-grandfather was a Scandinavian immigrant. Married an Italian girl." Mr. Elijah's whole face lit up and made him look younger when he talked about Walcott. "Used to live in a grand old house for seniors near the park at the center of town, but there was a real bad fire there last year. Whole block burned to the ground. Some of us seniors moved here to this new development."

Mr. Elijah looked really sad about having to leave the grand old senior citizens' home. I knew exactly how he felt. "Do you live here by yourself, Mr. Elijah?"

"Live with my daughter and her no-good husband. It was his idea to move here to this cookie-cutter development." Mr. Elijah wrinkled his mouth. "Can't say as I've gotten used to it yet."

I looked at Mama and Dad meaningfully. Mr. Elijah had been living here a whole year and still didn't like it. They both ignored me while Mr. Elijah told them about this thing that had happened in Walcott in 1943 and that thing that had happened in 1911. All that history put me to sleep in less than two minutes, but not before I'd made a promise to myself. For Mama's sake, I was gonna do what she asked. I was gonna try.

Chapter Six

Lillian's Pumpkin Soup

I was the first person off the bus when it arrived at school. I waved goodbye to Aeisha and Otis and hurried up the steps and into the building. Then I booked it up the stairs and turned the corner.

Great. Maria Poncinelli wasn't there yet.

I walked over to the wall outside our homeroom and leaned against it. There. Now all I had to do was wait for her to arrive. She would be so surprised to see me leaning against her wall that she would speak to me. Then I'd explain to her that I felt the same way she did about this school and this town. Soon we'd be hanging out together and leaning against walls all over town.

This trying thing was turning out to be hard work.

The day after my fall — or what Mama liked to call my tree-climbing fiasco — I had come up with a plan for fitting in at school. It was called Operation Pretend I Belong Here. For two weeks I tried to act like Aeisha by studying hard and behaving in school, but that just got me in more trouble.

The only people who noticed me were my teachers, and they expected me to keep it up! One teacher even mentioned putting me in the advanced classes! I knew I had to slack off or I'd be wearing owl glasses and joining the math club by the end of the year. So the next week I came up with another plan: Operation Smile If It Kills You. I went back to studying my usual way, though I kept trying to behave. But I added an extra-nice smile to everything I did. I smiled at people in my classes, in the hallways and on the bus. I remembered what Mrs. Gransby had told me about a smile being your passport. But my smile didn't even get me out the front door. For some reason, most everyone just looked back at me weird. Aeisha said my smile was more scary than friendly, but I ignored her. I couldn't understand why my plans weren't working. Finally I decided it was because I was thinking too big. Instead of trying to be friends with everybody, I would start with just one person: Maria Poncinelli.

I had seen her the other day when Mama and I were shopping in downtown Walcott. She was with her mother and three older sisters, and she stuck out like a neon sign. Her mother was all dressed up in a fancy pink suit, and her sisters were all wearing dresses and shoes with little heels. Maria was the only one wearing a bandanna and torn jeans, and she was walking a little behind them, like she didn't belong. I figured she would be a good person to make friends with, 'cause I knew how she felt. I didn't belong in this town or this school, either.

It didn't help that Aeisha was fitting in great at school. Mama had been right — people got tired of staring at us after just a few days. After that, Aeisha started making friends from her classes and joining clubs. She also had Otis. He was still following her around, except Aeisha was actually talking to him now. It turned out Otis was as much a superdweeb as Aeisha. He was taking advanced classes, too, and all he and Aeisha ever talked about was their homework and Davis. Davis was Otis's baby brother and just like Mrs. Spunklemeyer had told us, he kept his family awake all night crying. He said that 'cause of the baby, his mother hadn't slept in almost two months. Aeisha did some research on her computer on babies and gave him advice on how to make the baby stop crying. None of it had worked, but Otis still kept hanging around. I offered to train Grady to chase him away, but Aeisha said no. I figured that meant she liked Otis more than she was saying.

When I told Aeisha about my newest plan, Operation Two Rebels Are Better than One, Aeisha said the reason I wasn't making friends was because I had a big chip on my shoulder. She said I didn't really want to make friends. As smart as Aeisha is, she doesn't know what she's talking about sometimes. Why would I be going through all these plans *not* to make friends? And besides, this plan was gonna work—I hoped.

Standing there, leaning against the wall, I started to get a bunch of negative thoughts. Suppose Maria didn't want to be friends with me? What if she got offended that I was leaning against her wall? What if she got so mad, she wanted to beat me up?

I tried not to think about that.

I waited a few minutes. Other kids from our homeroom

looked at me on their way into the classroom, but no one said anything. Anna Banana walked straight into the classroom without even glancing at me. As soon as she and the rest of the school figured out that Aeisha and I weren't gangsters, she'd stopped being interested in me. I think she was actually disappointed.

After a few more minutes, I shifted and leaned with my back against the wall instead. I bent one knee and placed the sole of my foot on the wall. There. That was even cooler. I turned my head to look casually down the hall, and my foot slipped. Maria was coming!

I put my foot back up hurriedly and waited. I could feel my heart start to beat louder and faster. Maria appeared in front of me, and I could feel her checking me out. I swallowed quietly. She was dressed in her usual gear, except that her bandanna was blue this time. She looked at me for a few seconds with a blank face. Then she moved further down the wall and leaned there, too.

I started breathing again. This was great. Here we were, just two girls leaning against the wall and hanging out. I glanced at my watch quickly. The bell was going to ring soon, which meant we would have to start talking soon. If I was gonna risk getting a late slip, then I wanted it to be worth it.

I waited a couple more seconds and then turned to look at her. Maria didn't look like she was going to say anything. Maybe she was waiting for me to speak first.

"Hi," I said finally. I gave her a quick wave, too, and then the bell rang.

The last thing I noticed as Maria walked off with the

stream of other kids coming out of all the classrooms was a big smirk on her face.

By the time I got off the school bus that afternoon, I'd made up my mind. I wasn't going back to school again. Ever. Since we couldn't move back into our old neighborhood, Mama and Dad would have to get me a home teacher. I knew all about home teachers because of Daba, one of my old friends from Roxbury. Daba is a Muslim and is always dressed in those long, dark dresses that go all the way down to her feet, and she also wears a head wrap that looks like the ones nuns wear. She has a home teacher because there's something wrong with her heart and she's always sick.

I couldn't understand why my plan hadn't worked. I'd been leaning against the wall before our math class, just like I was earlier that morning. And just like in the morning, Maria had come and leaned next to me. And ignored me. This time there was no doubt about it. I had tried to talk to her a few times, but she hadn't answered me. She didn't even look at me.

I walked to our house automatically. Mama had put a big red clay pot with a fir tree on each side of the front door so I couldn't complain about not knowing which one was our house. Dad had said he would spell my name out on the grass if that didn't work. I unlocked the door to the house with my key and walked in. Everything was very quiet, as usual. Even Khatib was spending a lot more time at school than he used to. At dinner he was always complaining about how much his muscles ached—not from basketball practice but from dance class! Mama and Dad had started their new jobs and were really busy. Twice that week Dad hadn't even come home for dinner 'cause of some big project he was working on. He said all the hours he was putting in were expected of him, but I wondered how much of it had to do with him trying to show that he was just as good as those young hotshot engineers he worked with. Mama liked her new job, too. At dinner, she would talk about her students and their interesting projects. She even said that she enjoyed teaching. When she told us that, I knew we were stuck here forever.

As soon as I stepped inside the house, Grady came running into the hallway and stopped in front of me with his tongue hanging out. He knew that after school was our time together. I was trying to train him to do simple dog things, like sit, stay and fetch, from the dog-training book Mrs. Gransby had given me. The lady who had owned him before us had forgotten all about educating him, 'cause he didn't know how to do any of that stuff. "Hi, Grady. You wouldn't believe what happened to me today."

Grady gave me a short bark and started licking my hand. I got down on my knees and gave him a quick hug before peeling off my coat, gloves and hat. Then I looked him in the eye. Ms. Pitapat's book says you should always look your dog in the eye.

"Okay, Grady, sit!" I ordered loudly.

Grady licked my face again. His nose was wet and cold against my cheek. I pushed him away firmly. Ms. Pitapat's book says that you have to be firm with your pet.

"Sit!" I ordered again, trying to sound as mean as possible.

Grady just looked at me and wagged his tail.

"Pay attention, Grady." I put my hand on his back and pressed gently. "Sit, boy. Come on."

Grady turned around in a circle, knocking my hand off his back. He'd learned that all on his own.

"Sit. Come on, Grady, sit." I was begging now. I'd been trying to train Grady for two weeks and he hadn't learned one thing. At this rate, I was never gonna get to the cool circus tricks in the second part of the book. I knew I shouldn't be taking it so hard, but it seemed like nothing was going right that day. In fact, nothing had gone right since we moved here.

I decided to try and call Karen. Talking to her would make me feel better. When we first moved in I had spoken to Karen or Margarita almost every day. They missed me as much as I missed them. Then Mama got the phone bill and showed me that I had spent sixty-three dollars making phone calls to them in just one month! Mama had made me promise that I would only call once a week. I pulled our phone over to the stairs and sat down to dial. Grady came over and sat down by my feet.

"Sure, now you sit," I grumbled at him. The phone was ringing at Karen's house.

"Hello." I could tell Karen's little brother, Lucas, had answered the phone.

"Hi, Lucas, it's me, Ola."

"Ola who?"

I smiled, 'cause Lucas always does that when I call. He's a bratty kid — the kind that makes me glad I don't have any younger brothers and sisters. Normally I would have been yelling at him by this point, but even hearing his voice made me feel good. "Ola Benson."

"The Ola Benson who moved outta here weeks ago?"

"Lucas, get Karen for me," I ordered. Enough was enough.

"That Ola Benson?"

"Lucas!"

"No can do."

"No can do what?"

"Karen's not here, so you can't talk to her." Lucas laughed. "She went downtown with Margarita."

"Downtown?" I yelled. We'd never been allowed to take the train to downtown Boston by ourselves. Margarita, Karen and I used to always complain about that, 'cause downtown is the best place to go. That's where all the stores are, and the swan pond, and the park, which is called Boston Common, and vendors that sell popcorn, pretzels and pizza on the street. The three of us were always talking about how we couldn't wait until we were old enough to go by ourselves and how when we were sixteen we were going to get jobs at a department store downtown like Margarita's sister, Carmen. "Stop fooling around, Lucas."

"It's true," Lucas said. His squeaky voice sounded sad now. "Carmen took them ice skating, and Karen wouldn't let me go with her 'cause she said I bother her too much."

"Thanks, Lucas." I hung up quickly. They were probably forgetting all about me while they were having fun.

I stood up and put the phone back on the hall table. Maybe some food would make me feel better. The way I was eating Lillian's cooking, I was gonna have to add fat to my list of problems. Aeisha had even taken me aside because she wanted to talk to me about how I shouldn't use food to make myself feel better. She showed me pictures from one of her teen magazines of girls with eating disorders like anorexia nervosa and bulimia. They looked like normal girls to me, but when I told Aeisha that she just shook her head and said, "Exactly."

I walked into the kitchen and found Lillian there, as usual, in front of the stove. She was still dressing funny, and no one had said anything about it to her yet. That was probably because she was so quiet. Whenever Mama and Dad tried to talk to her, she never said much back. Marie-Thérèse had told us that she could speak some English, but it was hard to tell because she hardly said anything that had more than one syllable in it. It was really creepy. She was like a shadow. Dad said she just needed time to get used to living with us.

I could smell something delicious cooking, and I wondered what she was making. The day before, she had made us something called cod salad, which had salt fish and tomatoes and peppers in it. It was so good nobody could talk during dinner 'cause they were too busy eating. "Hi, Lillian."

"Ah-lo, Ola," Lillian said softly. She put a small bowl of some kind of orange-brown soup in front of me. It smelled good, but I wasn't feeling hungry anymore.

"No, thank you, Lillian," I said, pushing the bowl away from me a little. I put my elbows on the table and cupped my chin in my hands. If I'd been in my old neighborhood, I'd have been outside riding my bike or roller-skating — on the street.

I heard the sound of the bowl moving across the counter,

and I glanced down, surprised. Lillian had moved it back in front of me. I looked up and saw that she was watching me. "What?"

Lillian tapped my elbow with one finger and said, "*Manje*—eat," loud and clear.

I took my elbows off the counter. Lillian's voice always surprised me. It was deep and strong, like a cello. This was the first time she'd spoken to me without me speaking to her first. "I'm not hungry."

Lillian didn't take her eyes off me. Her voice came again, welling up from inside her. "Eat. Soup good inside you."

I picked up the spoon. "What kind of soup is this, Lillian?"

"Soup *jumeau,*" Lillian answered. She sat beside me on the other stool and started twisting her fingers in her lap. Finally she looked up and asked, "Is good?"

I nodded, taking another spoonful. Lillian's soup had made my appetite come back, but I was even more excited that Lillian was talking to me. I'd been wanting to ask her questions about Haiti, but Mama had made me promise not to pester her. "What's it made of?"

"Soup with . . . pumpkin," Lillian said slowly. "Is made with Walcott world-famous pumpkin."

I looked at Lillian. For a second there, she sounded just like Mrs. Spunklemeyer had on the day she'd brought us the pumpkin pie. I wondered if she was trying to be funny by imitating Otis's mama, but Lillian spoke again before I could be sure. "In Ayiti, we eat soup for first day of year."

"How come?" I asked. Lillian had a heavy accent that

sounded like French mixed in with something else. But her English was pretty good.

Lillian smiled a little. "Give you luck."

"But this isn't New Year's Day," I pointed out.

"I wish you for have luck." Lillian nodded.

I laid down my soup spoon and twisted around on my stool to look at her. Lillian had noticed me moping around the house after school. She had made the soup just for me. That was like something Mrs. Gransby would do. "Lillian?"

"Yes?"

"Can I ask you about where you lived in Haiti?" I asked politely. Mama couldn't say I was pestering if I got permission.

Lillian tilted her head and said, "Shoot."

I looked up, startled. Lillian was imitating Khatib. She sounded just like he did when he said that. Lillian had been watching us.

Lillian nodded. "Where I live in Haiti call Anse-à-veau."

"Ansahvo," I repeated, trying to say it like Lillian did.

"Anse-à-veau," Lillian corrected me.

"Is it pretty there?"

"Is small place. By the water—ocean. Is beautiful, the ocean."

"What do people do there?" I asked. I thought it would be great to live by the ocean. I'd go to the beach every day.

Lillian frowned. "Is poor place. Very poor. Most person make life on fish—catch fish, sell fish, eat fish. My *manman* sell fish for market. My sisters help Manman."

"How many sisters do you have?"

"I have three sisters. One is name Juliane, call Ju-ju. She fourteen. She say when she is big, she no eat fish no more. One is name Marie-José, call Ti Marie. She is nine like you and she love talk, talk, talk. Even when she is sleep, her mouth move. Last one is Edna, call Nou-nou. She is baby, four year, and always she hurry. She try to be born on road, when Manman come from market. She no like to wait for anything." Lillian shook her head and smiled.

I checked out Lillian's eyes. They had become less sad. I noticed that Lillian's English sounded better, too, the longer she talked. "Where did you learn English?"

"My friend Elise teach me. She learn English in school. I learn more when I in hospital." Lillian nodded. "I listen everything."

"You didn't go to school?"

Lillian shook her head. "I stop to help Manman with market."

"I thought everybody had to go to school. It's against the law not to go to school here," I said, frowning.

"Is why I come here, Ola," Lillian told me quietly. "Is hard life there for poor people. Get good job here. Send money for Ju-ju and Ti Marie school. Send money for them come one day."

"You don't want to go back?" I asked wistfully.

Lillian shook her head firmly. "No go back. Make place here for my family. Is better place. Is more job, more schools. More chance."

"I guess so," I said glumly. Those were the exact reasons why we'd moved to Walcott.

Lillian and I turned as we heard a big grunt and Khatib walked into the kitchen.

"Hi, Lillian. What's up, Ola?" he said tiredly. He was walking funny. He would take one step, stop for a second and moan, then take another step and start all over again. "What's wrong with Aeisha? She came in with me and she ran straight up the stairs."

I shrugged. "She probably went to study." Aeisha had been spending a lot more time in her room lately. Just as I had figured, getting her own room had made her even more of a hermit.

"Well, if it's that Otis who's bothering her, tell her I'll take care of him for her." Khatib struck his hand against his chest, like he was Tarzan. I rolled my eyes. It hadn't taken long for Khatib to start acting like he was God's gift to the world again. That was another sign that everybody was adjusting to Walcott but me.

"My legs," Khatib moaned. He finally made it to the counter and plopped down on one of the stools next to me. "This dance class is gonna kill me."

"I thought you only had dance class on Tuesdays and Wednesdays," I said to Khatib. Lillian had placed a bowl of soup in front of Khatib and left the kitchen. I watched her go, sorry that Khatib had interrupted us.

"I do," Khatib said quickly. He picked up his spoon and bent his face toward the bowl. "My muscles ache from yesterday's class — not that it's any of your business."

I raised my eyebrows. Khatib was acting weird.

"How's basketball practice going?" I asked.

Khatib shrugged and didn't say anything. Now I knew

there was something wrong, because Khatib loved to talk about how many points he scored in practice and how he was gonna single-handedly beat the next team they were playing.

"Don't you have a game coming up?"

Khatib nodded and kept eating his soup. I watched him for a minute, but I knew I wasn't going to be able to get anything out of him. Khatib is like a big clam. He won't tell anybody anything until he's ready. Why wasn't he talking? It had to be something to do with basketball. Maybe he'd had a really bad practice. Or maybe the coach had benched him for the next game.

I decided to leave him alone and go pester Aeisha. She would stay in her room studying until midnight if I didn't go up there and make her take a break. Besides, I wanted to run my plan for quitting school by her. She'd probably tell me it was stupid, but I'd get her to explain why and then I'd be prepared for Mama and Dad's objections. I stopped halfway up the stairs. I had stepped on something. I looked down and saw that it was a half-crumpled sheet of paper. It was one of Aeisha's test papers. Boring. I picked it up and smoothed it out anyway. It would give me a good excuse to barge into Aeisha's room.

Then I looked at it more closely and my mouth fell open.

It was a science test that she'd taken a couple of days before. Aeisha had gotten a C!

Aeisha never got C's. Aeisha never even got B's. She was a straight-A student—or she used to be. What had happened? She'd been studying like crazy since we started at our new school. Then I remembered how she'd been acting our first day of school. She'd been flipping through her books like she was worried. And ever since then she'd been studying double the amount that she used to.

I smoothed out the paper and tucked it into my back pocket. Just an hour earlier I'd been depressed 'cause I thought I was the only one not adjusting to this town. Now both Aeisha and Khatib weren't acting like themselves. I had been so caught up in my own problems, I hadn't even noticed theirs — which meant I wasn't acting like myself, either, 'cause I hadn't been keeping up with what was going on with the family. Somebody else had been doing that, though. Lillian. I realized now that she had made that big pot of good-luck soup for the whole family, not just for me. Just like Mrs. Gransby, Lillian was watching out for us.

Chapter Seven

The Weirdest Family Meeting Ever

T his neighborhood was full of weird people.

I turned the focus knob on Aeisha's binoculars to see if there was something wrong with it. Maybe I'd seen something that just *looked* like a lady throwing leaves all over her lawn. I looked again. Nope. It was a Saturday afternoon and there *was* a lady spreading leaves all over her lawn. She was an older lady, with curly white hair, and she was wearing a thick blue winter coat and blue rubber boots. She was dragging a huge garbage bag full of dead brown leaves and putting the leaves back on her front lawn. She would take a handful, toss them on the ground, move a little and then start all over again. I watched her for a few minutes. She was doing a good job of it, too. Soon her lawn would be covered with dead brown leaves.

I decided that she must be one of Mr. Elijah's friends from the senior citizens' home. She didn't look as old as the rest of his friends, but she sure would fit in with them. I'd met two more of Mr. Elijah's friends in the past two weeks 'cause he decided that he should introduce me to the neighborhood. First I'd met Mr. Portello, who thought he was a fortune-teller. He said he came from a stock of Gypsies that had come to Walcott in the 1920s and liked it so much they decided to stay. Then he read my palm and told me that I would grow up to be an important person in this town. Me? No way. I was getting out. Mr. Elijah told me that Mr. Portello held regular Saturday-night séances in his house — after ten o'clock. Otis told me later that Mr. and Mrs. Stern hated Mr. Portello because he spent a half hour of each neighborhood board meeting asking for permission to hold his late-night séances and they couldn't say no because that was how he made his living.

Then I'd met Mr. Arnold, the retired newspaperman. He was the founder of *The Walcott Sentinel,* which was the town newspaper. It was hard to talk to him because all he did was grill you with questions. When I'd gone to visit him with Mr. Elijah, he wanted to know who I was, when I moved here, what I moved here for, where I lived, and why I lived there. When I had answered all his questions, he barked out, "Headline: 'Newest Resident, A Real Nut.' " After meeting some of his friends, I told Mr. Elijah that *he* wasn't senile at all.

I lowered the binoculars to think for a minute. There weren't any rules against putting leaves on your lawn, but there was a recommendation about keeping your lawn neat and clean. I picked up the binoculars again and looked out at Otis's house. Yup, his bike was still there rusting on the lawn. That wasn't exactly breaking the rules, either, but it wasn't following them. Then I thought about Mr. Portello.

He followed all the rules about getting special permission for late-night visitors, but he followed them so well it made the Sterns mad. That was just as good as breaking the rules. If I hadn't known better, I would have thought there was something going on with the people in this neighborhood.

"Ola, what are you doing in here?"

I put the binoculars down and turned around. Aeisha was standing behind me with her hands on her hips.

"Aeisha, you wouldn't believe how weird our neighbors are."

"This is my room. That means you can't come in it without permission," Aeisha said, scowling.

"Don't have a cow, Aeisha. I just wanted to look outside your window." I was telling half the truth, anyway. My bedroom window looked over the backyard, and there hadn't been anything going on there. But I had also come into her room to see if I could find out more about Aeisha's grades. Aeisha would call that snooping, but I called it helping. As soon as I could figure out why Aeisha was doing so badly, I could come up with a plan to help her.

"You shouldn't be spying on people, anyway." Aeisha dropped her hands from her hips and walked over to her desk. She started pulling her schoolbooks together and packing them in her backpack. "It's rude."

"What's the matter with you?" I asked. Aeisha was super grumpy. I had a feeling all that extra studying wasn't working, 'cause the more Aeisha studied, the worse her attitude became.

"Girls!"

Aeisha and I jumped. Mama had burst into the room all

of a sudden and was standing there waving her arms up and down excitedly.

"Are you okay, Mama?" I asked.

"Family meeting. Now. In the living room. Let's go," Mama ordered. She looked really pretty in her red pantsuit and gold hoop earrings. She had gone to a luncheon for work earlier and she was still dressed up.

"I have to study, Mama," Aeisha protested. She had finished stuffing her backpack.

"It can wait a half hour. Let's go," Mama said again. She turned around and disappeared as fast as she had come in. Aeisha and I hurried after her. I figured it must be serious. We hadn't had a family meeting since we moved in here. That was because Dad hadn't been around enough to torture us with one. But here it was right in the middle of a Saturday afternoon and Mama was calling a meeting.

Khatib was already in the living room when we got there. He was stuffing his face with some of Lillian's *pate*. She had left them for us before going to her first English class that day. "Dad's not here. We can't have a family meeting without Dad," he said.

Mama shrugged and turned away. "We sure can."

Uh-oh. Khatib, Aeisha and I looked at each other. We knew Mama must be really mad with Dad to be shrugging him off like that. She had been upset earlier when Dad told her he couldn't go with her to the luncheon because he had to work.

"Somebody has to run this family," we heard Mama mutter. Aeisha and I sat down on the green-and-rose sofa. The new living room furniture had just been delivered the day before, and we hadn't had time to check it out yet. I bounced up and down on it. It was comfy.

"Now." Mama sat down on the tall wooden chair with the long arms. She looked like a queen, with her arms resting on the chair's arms and her back held straight. "Talk," she commanded.

"Talk about what?" Aeisha asked. She sounded nervous, but I bet I was the only one who knew why.

"About you — all of you. School. Home. Basketball. Your dad. I want to know what's going on with you all. It's been so quiet around here, it doesn't feel like home. Something must be up."

Aeisha, Khatib and I looked at each other again. Then we looked at Mama. I knew that Mama was right; something was going on with Aeisha and Khatib. But I also knew that Khatib would never admit it and that Aeisha would kill me if I told everyone about her grades. She would think I had been spying on her. Besides, I knew I wouldn't have to say anything for Aeisha. She always spills out all her problems at family meetings. Dad always starts with her at our meetings 'cause she's supposed to serve as an example for the rest of us.

I decided to speak up first. "I still think that it would be a good idea for me to quit school. I'm not really learning anything I couldn't learn at home and—"

"Ola, we already talked about that," Mama cut me off.

Shoot. I closed my mouth. I had talked over my idea for a home teacher with Mama early that week and she had said one thing: no.

"Khatib, how's basketball practice?" Mama asked, turning

to him. He had sprawled out on the floor on his back, resting on his elbows.

"No problem." Khatib nodded.

"Aeisha — your new classes?"

I looked over at Aeisha, waiting for her to spill it.

Aeisha heaved a big sigh.

Here it comes, I thought.

"Well," Aeisha said slowly, "I miss Dad. He's never around anymore."

"Yeah, me too," Khatib chimed in, sitting up. "He's like the Invisible Dad since we moved here."

Mama nodded. She looked really pleased with what Aeisha and Khatib were saying. Then she started to look sad. "I know. I've tried to talk to him about it."

"He hasn't asked me about basketball in weeks," Khatib said. "Not that I mind, that is."

I tried to keep my mouth from dropping. Khatib always minded when people didn't ask him how many points he had scored in a game or how well he had done in practice.

"He hasn't been around to check my homework," grumbled Aeisha.

Everybody looked at me.

"He was supposed to help me redo my star chart," I pitched in. This was the weirdest family meeting ever. Aeisha wasn't talking about her real problems and Khatib was shrugging off basketball. It was true that Dad hadn't been around much lately 'cause of work. We had all felt it. But it was like Aeisha and Khatib were using that as an excuse not to talk about other things.

"Your dad feels like he has something to prove in his new job," Mama explained, frowning.

" 'Cause he's black," Aeisha said, nodding.

"And because he's new and he's older than many of the other engineers in his position." Mama didn't sound like she was mad at Dad anymore.

"So what do we do?" Khatib asked, leaning back against one of the chairs.

"Maybe we should schedule an appointment with him," Aeisha suggested, pushing her glasses up on her nose.

Mama grinned at her. "Aeisha, child, you've got it."

"Got what?" I asked, confused.

Mama explained, "Maybe if we all start making family appointments with your dad, he'll start getting the point. We should all schedule time with him individually. Drive him crazy with it."

Aeisha, Khatib and I nodded and smiled back at Mama. This was gonna be fun.

Mama gazed at the three of us. She looked like she wanted to say more but thought better of it. Instead she raised her eyebrows and said, "Can I get a witness?"

We all laughed at her. That was always Dad's line at our family meetings. We all raised our hands and sang out, "Yeah."

"Then I guess we're adjourned." Mama sighed. I could tell that she knew something more was going on, but Mama never likes to push. That's Dad's department. He's more like me. He'll dig and dig until he finds out what is bothering one of us, and then Mama fixes it. These family meetings just don't work right without Dad.

I followed Aeisha out of the living room. I was worried about her now. Something really big must be happening for her not to have said anything about her trouble with school. And since Dad wasn't there, it was up to me to find out why she was keeping such a huge secret.

Aeisha turned around to look at me when we got to her room. "What, Ola?"

"What's the matter with *you*?" I asked, putting my hands on my hips. I was hoping that Aeisha would tell me what was wrong *before* I told her that I'd found her test.

"Nothing." Aeisha walked into her room and picked up her loaded backpack. It had so many books sticking out of it, she couldn't even close the zipper. Then I noticed that she was dressed up. She had on a jean skirt with a pink sweater and pink tights. She even had on shoes.

"Where you going?" I asked, moving toward her.

"Nowhere. And don't follow me," Aeisha ordered. I edged toward the window seat slowly. Aeisha's binoculars were still sitting there, and she hadn't said anything about not *watching* her.

"Where are you going?" Aeisha asked suspiciously.

I stood still. "To my room. I got homework to do, too, you know."

"Don't follow me, Ola," Aeisha ordered again. She gave me a look to say that she meant it, and then she walked toward the door. But before she got to the doorway, the zipper to her backpack slid all the way open and every single one of her books and papers spilled onto the floor.

She bent down and started picking them up fast. "Don't touch anything, Ola."

I didn't pay any attention to her. This was perfect. I'd been carrying her test paper with me for a few days, waiting for the right time to ask her about it. I pulled it from my pocket and let it float to the floor casually.

"Uh—Aeisha," I said quietly. She was stuffing the books back into her pack hurriedly.

"What?"

"You missed one." I pointed at the paper and widened my eyes. "Aeisha, you got a C?"

Aeisha ran over to pick up the paper. She stared at it, then crumpled it up and tossed it in the trash can by her desk. Then she went to sit on the edge of her bed. I walked over to her slowly. I hoped Aeisha wasn't gonna cry. Aeisha, Mama and I all have the Benson crying syndrome. One of us can't start crying without starting the other one off.

"So what's going on?" I reached over to pat her hand, just like Mama does when one of us is having a problem.

Aeisha snatched her hand away. "First you have to promise not to tell anyone—'cause I'm taking care of it."

"Okay," I promised. "Taking care of what?"

Aeisha hesitated. "I'm not doing so good in my science class."

"How come?"

Aeisha wouldn't even look at me. She was talking straight to her shoes. "I don't know. I guess I'm not smart enough."

I couldn't believe that. Science was Aeisha's best subject.

"It's the teacher." Aeisha spoke again, slowly. "I don't think he's grading me fair."

"How come?" I asked, standing up.

Aeisha shrugged one shoulder. "I don't know, Ola. I'm

studying harder than I've ever studied. I study until I know all the answers, but he always finds something wrong with them. I don't think he likes me. Our first day of school, he kept picking on me to answer questions—and I hadn't even got our science book yet."

I put my hands on my hips, mad. "What's his name?"

"Mr. Stillwell," Aeisha muttered. "That's not all, Ola. When I went to him for help, he said that he didn't think I belonged in the advanced class. He suggested that I go back to the regular science class."

"Aeisha, you gotta tell Mama and—"

"You can't tell anyone. I'm taking care of it." Aeisha stood up and went over to her backpack. She stuffed the last book back into it and zipped it up all the way.

"What are you gonna do?" I asked. Aeisha didn't look sad anymore. She looked angry.

"Otis is gonna help me." Aeisha slung the backpack over her shoulder.

"Help you do what?" I asked, following her as she headed toward the door.

"Catch Mr. Stillwell." Aeisha had a gleam in her eye that I'd never seen before. "Otis is in the same class as me and he always gets A's. We're gonna put each other's names on our tests, so Mr. Stillwell will think my paper is Otis's."

I was impressed. Aeisha had come up with a great plan. "But what about your handwriting? Won't he be able to tell? I'm coming with you."

"Otis and I are gonna practice each other's handwriting. I'm going over there right now to work on it," Aeisha said, going down the stairs. "You can't come."

I leaned over the railing. "Aeisha, if you need any help, just call me!"

Aeisha didn't answer me. I stared after her for a moment. I couldn't believe she had been going through all this stuff and hadn't told anybody about it. Aeisha was sure acting different since we moved here. Here I was trying to think up a plan for her for a whole week and she didn't even need my help. I decided to go look for Grady. He needed me. The two of us could take a walk over to Mr. Elijah's — maybe he would know why that lady was putting the leaves back on her lawn.

I whistled for Grady a couple of times and waited. Nothing. Grady didn't come running from one of our bedrooms or up the stairs. That was weird. I walked around upstairs and asked Mama and Khatib, but they hadn't seen him anywhere, either. Maybe Aeisha had taken him with her. I went downstairs to check around. If Aeisha had taken him out, she should have told me first. Grady was *my* responsibility. I walked around the front part of the house and then into the kitchen. Still no Grady. I stopped still when I heard a low voice coming from the backyard and then a short whistle. I walked over to the kitchen window. Lillian was in the backyard, all bundled up in Mama's old winter coat, and Grady was with her. I heard Lillian say something in Kreyol and watched in amazement as Grady started chasing his tail around and around in a tight circle. Then Lillian said something else, and he fell over on his back and stuck his legs in the air. He was playing dead.

Lillian was training my dog. And it was working! He was doing some of the circus tricks from the second part of Ms. Pitapat's book.

I watched them for a couple more minutes. I wanted to know how Lillian had taught Grady to do those tricks when he wouldn't even do simple things like sit or stay for me, but I also felt sort of mad. Even Grady didn't need me. Then I started to feel bad. Lillian was probably teaching Grady those tricks to surprise me. She knew how frustrated I was that he wasn't learning anything. Lillian was doing something nice for this family again.

I walked out of the kitchen and grabbed my coat and hat from the closet. I didn't want to ruin Lillian's surprise. I would go see Mr. Elijah by myself. When I went outside, the cold air hit me in the face and made it tingle. I walked down the street in the direction of the old lady's house, but I didn't see her anywhere. She had finished spreading out all her leaves, and you couldn't even see the brown grass of the lawn anymore. I looked at it for a couple of seconds. It was sort of pretty. The lady had even left a big pile of leaves in one corner that was perfect for jumping into.

I looked around. There would be nobody outside to see me.

Then I remembered my promise to Mama. I was supposed to behave myself better than that. The lady who lived in this house would probably report me.

I started walking again. When I reached Mr. Elijah's blue-and-white house, I saw that he was standing in his doorway with another man. Mr. Elijah noticed me and called out, "Just Ola! Exactly the person I want to see."

I had tried correcting Mr. Elijah about my name, but he didn't seem to understand. As I got closer to them, I noticed that the other man was much younger than Mr. Elijah and very short. He was also very red in the face. He looked embarrassed about something.

"Just Ola, this is my son-in-law, Mr. Julius Jones," Mr. Elijah introduced us cheerfully. "I was just telling him about your tree-climbing expedition. Again."

"Hi, Mr. Elijah. Hi, Mr. Jones," I said uncomfortably. I felt like I had interrupted something important. Mr. Jones had turned even redder when he found out who I was.

"H-How d-do you do," Mr. Jones stammered. He took a deep breath and looked at me steadily. He had nice brown eyes. "I'm very sorry about your accident."

"I'm okay now," I started to say, but Mr. Elijah cut me off.

"Ought to be ashamed of yourself," Mr. Elijah muttered, giving his son-in-law a hard look. "It's a crime, I tell you. A real crime to this town."

Mr. Jones ducked his head again. "Okay, Pop."

"Used to be a time when people were more free around here." Mr. Elijah wagged a finger at his son-in-law. "Until you came along."

I looked back and forth at them, confused. It was hard to believe this was Mr. Elijah's no-good son-in-law. He looked like such a nice man.

"I've got to go, Pop." Mr. Jones shuffled his feet nervously. "Please tell Janet I'll be home for dinner. Goodbye, Just Ola."

"You better be here on time, 'cause we won't wait on you," Mr. Elijah called after him. Mr. Jones scurried to his car and drove off quickly. "Come on in, Just Ola."

I followed him inside. "Mr. Elijah, what was that all about?"

Mr. Elijah grinned. He was wearing a blue flannel shirt and a baseball cap that said WALCOTT WARRIORS on it. "That was my no-good son-in-law, Just Ola."

"What's so bad about him?" I asked.

"Why, Just Ola, he's responsible for all of this." Mr. Elijah spread his arms wide and waved them up and down.

"For what?" I asked, looking around. All I saw was a nice hallway with a gray carpet and black-and-white photographs on the wall. Mr. Elijah's house was built just like ours, with the stairs in the front and the kitchen in the back. I didn't see anything out of the ordinary.

"For this neighborhood, Just Ola! He's the one that designed it," Mr. Elijah grumbled, leading me to the kitchen. He went to the pantry and pulled out a bag of lemon cookies.

"Really?"

"Went to some fancy architect school—Walcott College wasn't good enough for him." Mr. Elijah continued grumbling. "Came back home and built this cookie-cutter neighborhood."

I smiled at that. Mr. Elijah was right. The houses in this neighborhood did look like they had all been cut with the same cookie cutter. And Mr. Jones had designed them. No wonder Mr. Elijah had been giving his son-in-law such a hard time.

"And now," Mr. Elijah said in an injured tone, "he won't do anything about it."

I sat down at the wooden kitchen table. It had a pretty yellow gingham tablecloth on it. "But he doesn't look too happy either, Mr. Elijah."

Mr. Elijah grinned and plunked a plate full of cookies on the table. "That's because he's consumed with guilt. Want some hot apple cider?"

I nodded eagerly. "Mr. Elijah, I saw the strangest thing this morning. One of your neighbors was putting leaves back on her lawn."

Mr. Elijah picked up a large green pitcher. He brought it to the table and poured apple cider into two big green mugs. "That must have been Mrs. Angelo. She does like her leaves."

I picked up a cookie. "That doesn't make any sense."

Mr. Elijah sat down. "Makes plenty of sense, Just Ola. That neighborhood board has fixed it so they have a company that cleans up all the elderly residents' lawns. Mrs. Angelo woke up last week and found all the leaves on her lawn had disappeared. Came to the graybeard committee meeting sniffling and talking about leaf-stealing thieves. So we arranged to get her a few bags of leaves."

I took a small bite out of a cookie. The graybeard committee was the neighborhood senior citizens' club. Mr. Stern used to be in charge of it, but last year the other seniors voted him out and made Mr. Elijah president. "But Mr. Elijah, she put more leaves out there than she had before. You can't even see the grass anymore."

"She'll be jumping around in them later on, too," Mr. Elijah added.

I looked up. "But it's against the rules to play out in front of your house."

"That rule's for children. It doesn't say anything about

grown adults frolicking in some leaves." Mr. Elijah smiled slyly.

I stared at him for a minute. "Mr. Elijah, you all are breaking the rules in the neighborhood on purpose."

Mr. Elijah sat back in his seat and crossed his arms. "Not breaking them, Just Ola. Stretching them. If we stretch them so far they break once in a while, well, then we're real sorry."

I smiled. Mr. Elijah was just like me. He liked to shake things up, too.

"We could use a person such as yourself, Just Ola. To organize the kids in this neighborhood."

"Me?" I shook my head glumly. "I don't even know any of the kids in this neighborhood except Otis — and that's 'cause of Aeisha. I don't think they like me."

Mr. Elijah put his mug down. "That's 'cause they don't know you. Not a single one of them has the kind of fire you do, Just Ola. They need you around here to help them out. Shake things up a little."

I shook my head again. "I couldn't help even if I wanted to, Mr. Elijah. I'm restricted from using my planning powers. You saw how mad Mama was after my fall."

"Now, Just Ola, I'm surprised you'd let a little thing like parents stop you."

"Mama's no little thing, Mr. Elijah. And now that Dad isn't around as much, she'd probably be the one who'd end up punishing me. She'd probably pack me up and ship me to Greenland." I got to my feet. I didn't feel like talking anymore. It was making me feel bad that I couldn't help Mr. Elijah.

Mr. Elijah escorted me to the door. "The offer's good for a little while, Just Ola. You think about it."

I nodded and walked out the door. It was nice feeling like somebody needed and wanted me, but I didn't have to think about Mr. Elijah's idea. I couldn't help Mr. Elijah without any friends, and I didn't have any in this town. But there was more to it than that. I wasn't so sure I *wanted* to help. I hadn't realized it until that moment, but I was still hanging on to the hope that we might move back to Roxbury someday. If I made friends here in Walcott and helped to change the whole neighborhood, then I wouldn't have anything to complain about anymore. I'd really be stuck here. For good.

Chapter Eight

God's Gift to the World Can Dance

I got up bright and early on the next Saturday to get to the newspaper before Dad did. I dragged Grady down the stairs with me and opened the front door. Our rolled-up copy of *The Walcott Sentinel* was lying at the bottom of the stairs. It only came twice a week, since Walcott was so small it didn't have enough news to fill a daily paper.

"Fetch, Grady," I ordered, letting go of his collar. Seeing Grady do all those tricks the other day with Lillian had convinced me that some of my training must have finally sunk in with him. That was why Lillian had been able to get him to do those other tricks—I had already broken him in for her.

Grady perked up his ears and looked at me.

"Go get it!" I commanded, patting him on his back.

Grady looked at the newspaper and groaned.

"We're just gonna get colder sitting here with the door open," I said, shivering. I knew he could do it. "Come on, boy, fetch it!"

Grady sat down.

I sighed and ran down the stairs to get the paper. I was gonna have to ask Lillian what her secret for training Grady was. I lifted my head as I leaned down to pick up the paper. I could hear the faint sound of a baby crying. I figured it must be Davis, Otis's little brother. Poor Otis. That baby had to have some powerful lungs for me to be able to hear him. I looked across the street. I could see Mrs. Spunklemeyer standing in front of the windows on the second floor, holding the crying baby. She looked as tired as she had the day she dropped off the pie at our house. Aeisha said Otis was such a genius that he didn't have time to care about things like clothes and looking good, but I had my own ideas about that. I thought Otis's looking so bad had more to do with his mama. She was so tired from taking care of Davis that she didn't have time to see to Otis. Mr. Spunklemeyer was in the navy and was on a ship for six months, so Mrs. Spunklemeyer was taking care of Otis and Davis all by herself. I looked at her for a few more seconds before I picked up the paper and ran back into the house, where it was warm and comfortable. If we'd still been in our old neighborhood, I would have gone over there and helped Mrs. Spunklemeyer, but things were different here.

Grady barked and gave me one of his open-mouth dog smiles as I closed the door.

"You're useless, Grady," I lectured him, heading toward the kitchen. "You and me have to have a long talk about whose dog you are."

Grady whined.

When we entered the kitchen I saw that Lillian was already up, cooking breakfast. She was singing something under her breath that sounded like a church spiritual. I was glad to see she was in a good mood. She was dressed better, too, because Mama had taken her shopping for new clothes. But it wasn't just her new clothes that Lillian was happy about. She had been saving the money Mama and Dad paid her for working for us, and yesterday she had sent some of it home to her mother and sisters, along with a long letter written in Kreyol. I knew Lillian was happy that she could help her family. That was the main reason she had come to the United States, and it made her feel better about leaving her home.

"*Bonjou*, Lillian," I said in my best Kreyol accent. I climbed up on a stool and spread the paper out on the counter.

"Good morning, Ola," Lillian said slowly and formally. She was practicing her pronunciation. We had made a deal where I would help her with English and she would teach me Kreyol. Lillian liked her English class. She had even made a friend there who was from Romania, and they called each other on the phone all the time to practice speaking English.

Lillian walked over to put a plate of toast on the counter. There must have been fourteen slices of toast on the plate. Some of them were toasted light, some were medium, and some were almost burnt. Lillian must have gotten carried away with using the toaster.

"Thanks," I said. I was glad Lillian was in a good mood, but I was hoping she didn't expect me to eat all of that toast.

"What are you doing?"

I looked up and saw that Aeisha had come in, still wearing her pajamas and red bathrobe. She was barefoot, as usual. "I'm reading the paper."

"Since when did you start reading the news?" Aeisha squinted at the paper from behind her glasses. "Boy, you must be really bored."

I started to shake my head, then stopped. Aeisha was right. I was dying of boredom here in Walcott. That week had been especially bad. I'd given up on all my plans for school, and I'd stopped snooping on the neighbors now that I knew what they were up to. I was afraid that if I saw somebody else stretching a rule, I wouldn't be able to stop myself from joining in. I'd even kept away from Mr. Elijah so that I wouldn't be tempted. The only fun I did have was when Lillian had decided to keep me busy one day after school by teaching me how to cook. We had to hold our noses to eat the burnt rice, but everything else came out good.

Aeisha hopped up on one of the stools and took a piece of toast from the plate sitting in the middle of the counter. "Morning, Lillian."

Lillian looked over her shoulder and gave Aeisha a smile. "Good morning."

Aeisha dropped her toast.

"She smiled at me," Aeisha whispered, leaning toward me. "What did you do to her, Ola?"

I shrugged. The rest of the family was only just beginning to notice the change in Lillian. "I don't know. She's in a good mood or something."

Aeisha looked at Lillian one more time and picked up her toast. She took a tiny bite out of it. Aeisha even eats like an old lady. She has toast and coffee for breakfast every morning.

"Listen, Ola. Don't worry so much about school," Aeisha said in between bites of her toast. "You just gotta hang in there. Eventually people will learn to like you."

I thought about giving Aeisha a big kick in the shins but stopped myself. She had been in an even worse mood since she and Otis had switched their tests on Thursday. She was just taking all her nervousness out on me 'cause I was the only one who knew about it.

"Why don't you go over and help Otis? I heard Davis crying this morning," I suggested. I had promised myself that I would be super nice to Aeisha until she found out about her grade on that test. And I figured the best way to do that was to get her out of the house so I wouldn't end up breaking that promise.

Aeisha put her coffee cup down with a clatter. "What do you care about that?"

"Nothing. I just thought you might want to spend some time with Otis." I felt bad sending Aeisha off on another one of her missions to help poor Davis, 'cause I knew it wasn't gonna work. Aeisha doesn't know anything about babies. Not like me. I'd helped Mrs. Gransby baby-sit her grandkids lots of times.

I waited for Aeisha to say something smart back, but she didn't. I looked up and saw that she had her head down, practically in her plate. Aeisha actually looked embarrassed! And all because I had mentioned Otis's — "Oh, no, Aeisha. Not Otis!"

Aeisha's eyes blinked quickly, and then I knew for sure

that she was hiding more than just her science grade. Aeisha had a crush on Otis, of all people!

"He's not so bad," Aeisha said quickly.

I nodded slowly. Reading all those romance novels must have made Aeisha's brains turn to mush. I should have known something was wrong with her when she started talking to Otis. It wasn't just that he was a dweeb; she actually liked him. Gross.

I had to get out of there before I started laughing. I didn't think that would qualify as being super nice. I ran out of the kitchen, holding my mouth, and bumped straight into Dad. "Hi, Dad. What are you doing home? It's Saturday, you know."

Dad blinked sleepily. He looked tired. "Fresh."

I tugged on one of his hands. "Don't forget our appointment tonight. Eight o'clock. I have a lot to talk to you about."

Dad nodded. "For your information, I have you down in my book, Ayeola. And I'm home because I have an appointment with Lillian this morning."

"Lillian? Really?"

"Yes, I have an appointment with her great coffee." Dad yawned. "If I don't get some soon, I'm gonna pass out, hear?"

I stepped out of the way quickly and moved to sit on the stairs. Dad had been really good about keeping all our appointments, even if it meant leaving work and then having to go back. Mama said that the plan hadn't worked the way she had hoped but that this was a nice compromise.

"Out of my way, Ola."

I looked up and saw Khatib on the stairs, bundled up in

his winter coat and wearing his sweatpants. He was carrying a small black bag, but it wasn't his gym bag.

I moved over a little so Khatib could pass. "Going to basketball practice?"

"Yeah," Khatib mumbled, heading toward the front door.

"Well, where's your basketball sneakers? Where's your gym bag?" I asked loudly. It was strange that Khatib would have forgotten those. He took them to every basketball practice.

Khatib shrugged and pulled on his gloves. "Don't need them today. See ya later."

I ran to go look outside through the picture window. Khatib hadn't even blinked at my questions, but that didn't mean they weren't good questions. How could he be going to basketball practice without his sneakers? Unless maybe he wasn't playing. Maybe the coach had benched Khatib for some reason. But that wasn't the only strange thing. Not only was Khatib going to basketball practice without his sneakers, he was also going there at least an hour late. Practice started at seven-thirty every Saturday. I ran to the closet and pulled on my coat quickly. This was just what I needed to keep me busy. Maybe I could figure out what was going on with Khatib by watching his basketball practice. I ran outside just in time to see him turn the corner and disappear. Luckily, there were plenty of trees and bushes in this neighborhood that I could duck behind, so I could follow Khatib without him catching me. For once I was grateful that I didn't know everybody in the neighborhood, or else somebody would have called out my name and blown my cover.

I followed Khatib for four blocks, slowly. He was walking in the direction of the main road, where the bus stop was. I made sure that I stayed way behind him so he couldn't see me. Finally I saw him stop at the bus stop, which was in front of a big stone church. I stopped and ducked behind a huge statue at the side of the church. Khatib was peering at the bus schedule.

Next time I would remember to bring Aeisha's binoculars, I told myself. This was just like being a spy, and I thought I was pretty good at it 'cause Khatib hadn't caught me yet. I wondered if this would be a good career for me: Ola Benson, private eye. Spies got to do all sorts of unusual things. I poked my head out from behind the statue and froze suddenly. Khatib was walking right toward me!

I huddled behind the statue and tried to make myself as small as possible. I hoped he just wanted to look at the statue and wasn't coming over to yell at me. I waited quietly for a few seconds. Then I waited for a few more. I didn't hear the sound of Khatib's shoes or the rustle of his jacket or anything at all. I peered out from the side of the statue at the bus stop, but Khatib wasn't there! Where was he? I hadn't heard a single bus pass by yet. I scurried to the other side of the statue and peeked around the other side. Khatib was nowhere to be seen.

"What are you doing?"

I jumped back and hit my head on the statue, hard. "Oww!"

"You okay?"

I nodded slowly. My eyes were still blurry with tears of pain, but my ears were working fine. It wasn't Khatib who'd

found me behind the statue. I blinked the tears away quickly and looked with surprise at the person in front of me. It was Maria Poncinelli — bandanna, torn jeans and all.

"You sure?" she asked, fiddling with the zipper of her jacket. She was wearing a big black leather jacket, and her hair was pulled back into a ponytail that was tucked inside her coat.

I nodded again and touched the new lump on the back of my head. I was gonna have to rethink my career as a spy. First I lost the person I was following, then I let someone sneak up on me.

I looked at Maria Poncinelli carefully. It was the first time she'd ever talked to me. Her voice was surprisingly nice. I'd thought it would be gruff and deep — to match her attitude. Instead, it was kinda high and musical.

Maria came forward and leaned one shoulder against the statue. There it was. The attitude. I was impressed.

"So what happened to you?" she asked casually. "You haven't been leaning against any walls lately."

"I've had stuff on my mind." I shrugged. I was surprised Maria had even noticed. "I figured you could hold up the wall all by yourself."

Maria shook her head seriously.

"Just don't give my place to anyone else," I joked, leaning against the statue too. Maria didn't smile, and I wondered if it was because a smile would ruin the effect of her attitude or because she didn't have a sense of humor. I considered passing on Mrs. Gransby's advice about your smile being your passport but decided against it. She'd probably think I was stupid.

124

"You go to church here?" I asked, waving my hand in the direction of the church. My shoulder was starting to feel cold from where it was resting against the statue.

Maria nodded and looked bored. "My sisters are in there."

"Yeah?"

"Antoinette and Careen."

"Your sisters?" I nodded, shifting my weight to my other leg. "How come?"

"I'm supposed to be in there, too." Maria frowned. She looked like joining her sisters was the last thing she wanted to do. "Stupid dance class."

"Huh?" I stood straight, forgetting all about my attitude. I remembered Khatib.

"Mrs. Felix's dance class. They have it in the basement every Saturday and Thursday," Maria informed me.

"For school?"

Maria looked at me like I was a dodo head. "You have to sign up for this class. Pay money. Mrs. Felix used to dance on the stage, and she's the best dance teacher in Walcott."

I leaned my whole body against the statue now. Khatib hadn't been walking toward me earlier; he had been walking into the church. He wasn't going to basketball practice; he was going to dance class! Voluntarily!

"Mrs. Felix is nuts," I heard Maria say.

"She is?"

"She must be crazy to come live back here after living in New York." Maria shook her head.

"Yeah," I mumbled, barely listening to her. Khatib was always complaining about having to take those dance classes at school. But here he was taking dance classes outside of school when he was supposed to be at basketball practice. Why was he keeping this such a big secret? "Hey, is there any way you can see in there without going inside?"

Maria nodded. "There's a window in the back of the church."

I started walking around the church quickly. To my surprise, Maria followed me, walking at her own pace. The back of the church had a small parking lot that was full of cars. Mrs. Felix's dance class must be really popular. I found the window Maria had told me about and bent down to peer into the basement of the church.

At first I couldn't make out anything. The basement was full of people, mainly girls dressed in tights and leotards and moving all around the room. From the quick way they were moving I could tell this wasn't a ballet class, like the one I used to take at the community center. It looked like a modern-dance class.

"That's Mrs. Felix," Maria told me. She had bent down beside me and was looking inside, too. She was pointing to a short, round lady with curly red hair.

"She used to dance on the stage?" I asked. Mrs. Felix sure didn't look like a dancer. She was about fifty years old and chubby all over.

"That's what happens when you come back to Walcott," Maria said with a twist of her lips. She looked really disgusted. "That who you're looking for?"

I looked in the direction where Maria was pointing and saw my brother, Mr. God's Gift to the World, in a corner with three other boys. Khatib was the tallest of the three and stuck out 'cause he was the only one not wearing tights. He had on a pair of cutoff sweatpants and a sleeveless T-shirt. He and the three other boys were rehearsing some move where they ran three steps, jumped, then twisted in the air, landing with one foot on the ground and one way up in the air behind them. I watched them do it over and over again, expecting Khatib to fall and break his leg at any minute, but he didn't. Khatib did the move right every time. He was really dancing.

"That your brother or something?" Maria asked me.

"Or something," I said. This person looked like Khatib, but he sure wasn't acting like Khatib. My brother would never give up basketball for dance lessons. Khatib had never even shown any interest in dancing. I thought about that and realized that it wasn't exactly true. It was Khatib who used to walk me to the community center to take my ballet class every week, and most of the time he stayed until it was over so he could walk me home again. But he used to complain backward and forward about it. Had Khatib been interested in dancing back then, too?

I watched Khatib for a few more minutes until the shock wore off, then I straightened up. I wasn't going to get any answers from staring at Khatib. I glanced at Maria, who was standing beside me and looking across the parking lot. I'd been so busy thinking about Khatib that I hadn't realized I was having an actual conversation with Maria.

"So," I said finally. I leaned back against the church.

"So." Maria leaned back, too.

"Your dad's the mayor, huh?"

"Yeah, right." Maria's lips started quirking at the corners. "My dad couldn't run this town. He sells insurance."

I frowned, wondering if that girl River had given me the wrong information on the first day of school. "Your dad's not the mayor?"

"Heck, no." Maria had stopped laughing and was looking sort of depressed now. "My mom is. I don't like to talk about it."

"How come?" I asked. I thought it was kind of cool that Maria's mom was the mayor.

"You ask a lot of questions." Maria frowned. She turned her head away again to look across the parking lot. I tried doing the same thing, but there wasn't anything to look at except a bunch of parked cars and the fence that went around the back of the church. I was bored within seconds.

I turned back to Maria. "Listen, I need kind of a tour guide."

"Tour guide?" Maria repeated, lifting one of her eyebrows.

"You don't want to go to dance class and I don't have to be anywhere," I explained, burying my hands in my pockets. "I need somebody to show me around Walcott so I can figure some things out about it. You could give me your own personal tour of this town."

"My own personal tour?" Maria's lips were quirking up at the corners again. I wondered if she was laughing at me.

"Yeah."

Maria's eyebrow came down, and she straightened up and nodded. "Okay, Benson. Just let me go in and tell my sisters. My mom will have a cow if she thinks I've disappeared."

Chapter Nine

The Dead of Walcott

Maria's idea of a first stop on her tour was the cemetery in downtown Walcott.

I stood at the edge of the grass, looking at all the graves nervously. All of a sudden this tour didn't seem like such a great idea. I'd meant for Maria to show me the town of Walcott, not the dead of Walcott. I'd never even been in a graveyard before. Lots of scary stuff was supposed to happen to you in cemeteries. I didn't like how quiet and dark it was. The further we got from the road, the darker it had become. The only noise around was the sound of Maria's shoes crunching on leaves and sticks.

"These are the people who've gotten out of Walcott," Maria announced, walking around the different-sized headstones.

That was fairly obvious.

"Come on." Maria stopped and turned back to look at me. She was taking her tour guide duties very seriously.

I walked forward slowly. This graveyard was chock-full of

dead people. There were headstones of all kinds squeezed in close together. Some were made of shiny, polished marble; others were just pieces of rotting wood. As I walked I noticed dates like 1811, 1868, 1922 and 1967. People had been dead in here for forever.

"This is the only graveyard in Walcott. Everybody in this town has family here," Maria informed me. She stopped in front of a plot that had only a white wooden cross for a marker. "This is one of the oldest cemeteries in the state."

Oh, brother. It looked like Maria was turning into another person who was gonna give me a history lesson about Walcott. I already had heard enough about this town to write a book about it. "Is that what you wanted to show me? One of the oldest cemeteries in Massachusetts?"

"Who cares about that?" Maria moved on and stopped in front of a huge gray-and-white marble headstone. "These are people who've gotten out of Walcott. That's what's important."

I swallowed. "But they had to die to do it."

Maria shrugged. "You gotta get your inspiration where you can, right?"

I wasn't so sure about that.

"When I get out of here, I'm not coming back like Mrs. Felix—I'm getting out for good," Maria announced. She said it right to the gray-and-white headstone. "Right, Granny?"

I jumped and looked around, expecting to see some little white-haired old lady standing nearby. But there was no one around except us. I moved a little so I could see the words written on the headstone. It had MARIA ALICIA PONCINELLI carved on it in large, fancy letters. Below it, in smaller letters, was BELOVED MAYOR, MOTHER AND WIFE. "That's your grandmother?"

Maria nodded.

"She was mayor, too?"

Maria nodded again. The depressed look was back on her face again. "I'm supposed to be the next one."

My mouth dropped open. "You are?"

Maria sighed. "It's a tradition. The youngest daughter in each generation."

I closed my mouth. I had a whole new understanding of Maria Poncinelli. "Well, maybe your mama will have another baby."

Maria shook her head. "She wants to. But my dad's not cooperating. He says I'll have to do."

I didn't know what to say to that. It must be terrible to have your whole life planned out for you. No wonder Maria wanted to get out of here. She felt as trapped in this town as I did.

"Come on." Maria turned around and led the way out of the cemetery. Soon we were standing in the town center, if you could call it that. Walcott's idea of a downtown was two cobblestone streets with all these little boutiques and small shops on it. There wasn't a big department store like Filene's or J. C. Penney. There wasn't a swan pond. And there weren't any vendors selling popcorn, pretzels or pizza. Downtown was like stepping back in time fifty years.

I had to admit that the buildings were interesting, though. They all looked real old. Some of them were made of clapboards. Some of them were made of brick, and others were made of stone. They were old, but they all looked like they were well taken care of. The other thing that I noticed were the houses around the town. They were old, too, but they were all different from each other. Each of them had a different design and different colors. They were much closer together, and the streets were so narrow, you could barely fit two cars in the road at the same time. It was totally different from where we lived.

"This is it," Maria said, stopping in front of one of the small shops on the street. The shop had long white curtains in the windows, so you couldn't see inside. There was a small white sign that had WALCOTT THRIFT SHOP painted on it in fancy black letters. "This is where you can find all the stuff that belonged to people who got out of Walcott."

As we stepped through the doorway a bell jingled above us, but it didn't look like there was anybody minding the store. I looked around at the racks of clothes and shelves of books, kitchenware, and other stuff. "Wowww."

The thrift shop had some really old stuff in it. There was one whole rack full of military uniforms. Each one was labeled with what war it was used in. They had uniforms from the Civil War, the Spanish-American War, and World Wars I and II, and even one uniform as late as the Vietnam War. Another long rack was full of fancy party dresses made of silk, taffeta, and even polyester. There were clothes that farmers, millworkers, firefighters and judges would wear in different time periods. Way in the back I even noticed a couple of old Pilgrim-looking clothes. In Boston, this place wouldn't have been called a thrift shop. It would have been called an antique shop.

"People just donate all this stuff when they die?" I asked, walking over to where Maria was standing by a really old-looking wooden telephone and a pair of crutches.

Maria shrugged. "What else are they gonna do with it?"

"In Boston, all this stuff would be in a museum," I told her. Maria was fiddling around with the telephone. "So this is where you're gonna donate all your stuff when you leave here?"

Maria nodded. Her bandanna was coming loose and sliding down her forehead. She pulled it back into place. "Yup."

I nodded. "How come no one's in here watching all this stuff?"

Maria put the phone down and headed toward the door. "'Cause no one ever buys anything here. They just donate. Come on, I'll take you to the ice cream parlor. They have the best maple ice cream. They only make it here in Walcott."

"All right." I was starting to enjoy this tour of Walcott now that I could understand the theme. "And that'll probably be the last thing you eat before you get out of here, right?"

"Right." Maria actually smiled. Funny, I hadn't seen Maria's attitude since we left the church. I had a feeling that the bandanna, the torn jeans and the attitude were all part of some twisted plan of Maria's to keep people from thinking of her as the next Poncinelli mayor of Walcott. And it was working, 'cause even I didn't believe she could be a responsible citizen dressed like that.

"What's that?" I asked, pointing. Way out behind what looked like some woods, I could see a cloud of dust rising. I could also just make out what sounded like machines running at a construction site.

Maria looked to see where I was pointing. "That's Walcott Corners II," she said as we reached the ice cream parlor.

I wasn't surprised to see that it was one of those old-fashioned ones with a soda fountain and booths and a long counter with high stools around it. So far nothing in Walcott looked modern—except for Walcott Corners. "I don't get it."

Maria waved her hand at the guy who was standing behind the counter. I guessed that she came here so often, they knew just what to bring her. "Don't get what?"

She sat down in one of the long booths near the window and immediately crossed her legs and put her feet up at the end of the table. The attitude was back. I figured it was because we were in public again.

I told Maria about the millions of rules for living in Walcott Corners, and how the houses all looked the same, and how Mr. and Mrs. Stern were always watching people like they were the police, and all the other stuff that bothered me about living there. "I just don't get why a town that's so crazy about its history would let them build a place like that."

Maria shrugged. "It brings money and people into the town. My mom says that the new houses they're building will bring lots of revenue in."

"Yeah, but what do you need the money for?" I was confused. Walcott might be an old town, but it didn't seem like a poor town to me. Their schools had swimming pools and tracks and football fields. They had plenty of restaurants and parks. There was hardly any crime, judging by the fact that Otis's bike had been rusting away on his lawn for almost two

134

months now. And the other thing I had noticed was that there weren't any homeless people in Walcott. In downtown Boston, you see homeless people everywhere, begging for money or just living on the streets.

"You can always use more money. Put it in the school fund or the arts fund. It takes a lot of money to keep this town looking good." Maria sounded like she knew what she was talking about.

"Yeah, but what about all your history and town character?" I asked.

Maria frowned. "I guess I see what you mean."

"And it's not like they can't make the money some other way. You could open up two museums with all the stuff in that thrift shop. You could charge admission to go to that graveyard. All those old graveyards in Boston are big tourist places." I told Maria about all our field trips to places like Salem, where they had held the famous witch trials, and Bunker Hill, where they had fought that famous battle, and the oldest meeting house in downtown Boston, which had been the center of the abolitionist movement. I hadn't even known I remembered all that stuff so well. I guess I had been paying more attention during those school field trips than I'd thought.

The guy from behind the counter finally arrived with our ice creams just as I finished talking. He was wearing a white uniform and a white cap. I noticed that he had a bunch of red pimples on his face and long, greasy blond hair. Gross.

"Two maple ice creams." He sighed, putting two big sundae glasses on the table. "Maria—you hafta take your feet off the table."

"Go away, Curtis. I'm thinking," Maria said, ignoring him. She did look like she was thinking hard about something. Her eyebrows were close together as she concentrated.

"You hafta, Maria—what if my dad walks in here?" Curtis shifted from one foot to the other nervously.

Maria sighed and moved her feet back under the table. She picked up the long sundae spoon and dug into her ice cream. "You're such a baby, Curtis."

Curtis turned and walked back to the counter slowly.

"Who's that?" I asked Maria, digging into my own ice cream.

"That's Curtis. His family's owned this place since 1945." Maria leaned forward. "He hates working here. He'd rather work at the supermarket with his girlfriend."

"Oh." I nodded.

"You should do something," Maria announced suddenly. She put her ice cream spoon down.

"About what?" I asked, surprised.

"About Walcott Corners—about all those rules." Maria slapped her hand on the table. I looked at her, a little afraid now. She looked sort of mad. "If it's like you say it is, and all the neighbors are as unhappy as you are, then all of you should do something."

"Some of them are." I told Maria about Mr. Elijah and the graybeard committee, but I didn't tell her about what Mr. Elijah had asked me to do. I was trying to forget all about that.

"But you have to do more than that. It has to be bigger than just your neighborhood, 'cause they're building another one right now." Maria was nodding slowly. "You have to do it right. There's a whole process to these things, you know. You start with a petition. In government, they always want to see a petition before they change anything."

"How do you know so much about this stuff?" I asked, curiously.

Maria shrugged. "I used to hang around my grandmother's office when she was mayor. She let me sit in on all her business meetings, and then afterward she would explain to me what was going on. That was before she died. My mom never lets me do any of that stuff. She thinks I'll embarrass her 'cause I wear ripped jeans and tie-dyed shirts."

I swallowed my last bite of ice cream. Maria was right about the ice cream. It was really good.

"Think about it." Maria pushed the dish away from her and stood up. "I can even be your political advisor. Since I know about this stuff, I might as well help you. You ready?"

I started to slide out of the booth. "Where are we going next?"

"The train station."

"How come?"

"'Cause that's one of the few ways to get out of Walcott."

For the rest of the morning, Maria took me to the train station, the bus station and the taxicab office. I wasn't even surprised to see that the train station had an old steam engine that was one of the first trains ever built in the United States and that the taxicab office had a bunch of great photos of when they used to drive horses and buggies in Walcott. Maria showed me all the best routes for getting out of Walcott and told me how much each escape route would cost. I found out it would only cost me twelve dollars to catch a bus to downtown Boston and that they even showed a movie on the bus. The train was faster but way more expensive. Maria had getting out of Walcott all figured out. As she showed me around she kept dropping hints to me about how to get things changed at Walcott Corners. She said there would be a town hall meeting the next week and that it would be a perfect time to present the petition, and she talked about drawing up plans to bring new revenue into the town in other ways, like having a museum. She was sure the town committee would really go for that. Most of what Maria was saying went way over my head. I didn't know anything about politics and petitions, but I could tell that she was really excited about it.

"I don't know, Maria. Why don't you do all that stuff, since you know so much about it?" I said finally.

Maria stopped. We were on our way back to the church so Maria could meet her sisters. She hesitated. "It'd be better if it came from someone living in Walcott Corners. Besides, I wouldn't want anyone to get the idea that I *like* this town."

"Well, me either," I pointed out.

Maria shifted her weight from one leg to the other. She looked uncomfortable. "My grandmother wouldn't like it if she knew the stuff that was going on at Walcott Corners. She used to have all sorts of plans for improving the town, too — in a good way."

We stood on the sidewalk outside of the church silently for a few seconds. I don't think either of us was sure what to say. We'd spent most of the morning together, but now that it was over, it was kind of awkward.

"Thanks for the tour," I said finally. I knew I was going to have to get going soon. Khatib would kill me if he found out that I knew his secret.

"See ya later, Ola." Maria nodded and started walking toward the front door of the church. She turned around when she was halfway up the sidewalk. "Remember what I said about the petitions. I wouldn't mind helping you."

"Yeah," I said, nodding too. "I'll think about it."

As I walked home I realized that my thoughts were all jumbled up. I had made my first friend in Walcott, and I felt good about that. But I didn't know how to feel about anything else. I had learned a lot about this town during Maria's tour, and I realized that it wasn't such a bad place. I knew more about the neighbors now, too, thanks to Mr. Elijah, and they didn't seem so strange anymore. In fact, if you looked at it a certain way, I guess you could call them unusual. Just like me. But didn't joining in and helping out the neighborhood mean saying goodbye to Karen, Margarita and Mrs. Gransby forever? We had moved here only two months before and already I felt like all my memories of the old neighborhood were slipping away. I hadn't even talked to Karen and Margarita in weeks. Maybe they were forgetting about me, too. The more I thought about it, the more I realized that things had changed whether I liked it or not. We really weren't going back to the old neighborhood. And if we weren't going back, was this the kind of place that I wanted to live in?

Chapter Ten

Ola Joins Forces

I told Maria on Monday that I was going to go ahead with her idea of getting things changed at Walcott Corners and in the town.

"On one condition," I added, leaning against the wall outside of homeroom. I had found Maria there as usual, attitude in place.

"What's that?" Maria asked, narrowing her eyes. She was trying to look mean, but I could tell she was interested.

"I'll do the petition stuff and work to get things changed with the neighborhood association, but you have to do the proposal for the museum and all that extra-revenue stuff. I don't know anything about that." I held my breath. I had the feeling Maria was going to be as reluctant to work for the town as I had been to work for my neighborhood. But I had another feeling that told me Maria cared more about this town than she wanted anybody to know. She cared about this town the same way she told me her grandmother had.

Maria didn't answer me for a long time. I waited even after the bell rang. Finally she looked at me and nodded. "Okay."

"Okay," I replied, inching toward the classroom door.

"Where you going? We got work to do, plans to make," Maria told me, moving away from the wall. There was a new light in her eyes that made me really glad I was on her side of this fight.

"I've gotta get inside, Maria. I'll meet you after school. We can go to my house." I hurried inside the classroom, hoping Mrs. Woodstein hadn't taken attendance yet. Maria might not mind staying after school for detention, but I did.

I stayed in the lunchroom instead of going outside so I could think about my part of the plan. I still had to go over to Mr. Elijah's and tell him that I was taking over the kids' part of what I was now calling Operation Shake It Up. I would have been thinking with Maria, but we didn't have the same lunch period.

"Ola." I looked up and found Aeisha and Otis standing in front of me. They were smiling and holding hands. Yuck.

"What?" I asked, trying not to look at their hands.

Aeisha sat down beside me and pushed her glasses up on her nose. I noticed that she was wearing blue eye shadow. "We got our tests back."

I looked back and forth from Aeisha to Otis. "And?"

"Otis got an A and I got a C. Isn't that great?" Aeisha smiled.

"That's great, Aeisha." I was really happy for her. Now maybe she would stop being in a bad mood and start acting like her regular nerdy self. "But what are you gonna do now?"

Aeisha frowned. "Otis and I have to tell Mama and Dad. They'll probably want to talk to the principal."

"That'll get Mr. Stillwell," Otis muttered. He was looking at his test paper and scowling. He'd probably never gotten a C before, either.

Aeisha stood up. "We gotta go tutor. Will you tell Mama I'm gonna help Otis baby-sit his little brother after school?"

I nodded and tried not to watch as they grabbed hands again and walked away. I guess I was gonna have to get used to that too. I was proud of Aeisha, though. She had a lot of guts to try and handle her problem with Mr. Stillwell all on her own. Mama and Dad would probably be mad that she hadn't come to talk to them first. But maybe that would take the heat off of me. I was about to break my promise to be-have — in a big way.

I started to think about my plan again. The first thing I had to do was to get recruits. I could work a lot faster get-ting those petitions if I had more people to help me go around the neighborhood. Besides Maria, I knew I could count on Aeisha, Otis and —

"Hi."

I looked up and there was that frizzy-hairdo girl again. River. The one who'd talked to me the first day of school. She put her lunch tray on the table and sat down across from me. I wondered why she was still inside eating lunch. The only people left in the lunchroom were a few kids do-ing their homework or getting tutored. And I wondered why she had decided to sit with me. I hoped she wasn't going to ask me any more stupid questions.

"Hi," I mumbled, waiting to see what she wanted.

"You're looking pretty normal these days."

"Huh?" I asked, confused. "What do you mean?"

"I mean you're not wearing your I'm-an-ax-murderer smile and you don't sit in the front of the class in math and history anymore." River sipped her milk through her straw and stared at me with her watery blue eyes.

She was right. River had noticed that I had given up on my plan to make everyone like me at this school. I had stopped giving everyone my friendly smile on the bus and in class. I had stopped behaving extra good, too.

"Listen, I'm not up for any more of your dumb questions," I said, deciding to ignore what she'd said about my friendly smile. Did it really look like an ax murderer's smile? That was kinda funny.

"Okay." River shrugged and started to unwrap her sandwich.

"Okay?" I repeated, surprised.

"Okay." She nodded. "You were right, they were dumb. My dad says you should never make assumptions about people."

Neither of us said anything after that. River concentrated on eating her food, and I stared at the green walls and thought about what she'd said. She sounded like she had meant it. I glanced at her and then back at the wall. Just maybe she was an okay person. She looked okay. She was dressed in purple overalls and a black turtleneck.

"So how come your name is River?" I asked casually, taking my eyes off the walls.

"Look, I wouldn't talk if I were you, Ay—Ayeola."

I tried not to smile. "My name's African. My mother gave us all African names. Mine means 'born to kill.' "

River laughed, and the milk she was drinking started running from her nose.

"Gross," I said, handing her some napkins. This time I did smile.

River mopped her nose and smiled back. "Is that what your name really means?"

"No. I made that up."

"Well, mine's a granola name. You know—hippies. My dad was really into meditation and yoga and peace stuff and eating raw vegetables before I was born." River shook her head.

"Does he still do that stuff?"

"Well, my baby brother's name is Broccoli."

I laughed, 'cause I could tell she wasn't serious. I was starting to like this girl. "What's his real name?"

"Philip. And my dad eats steak now. It was just a phase." River picked up her sandwich and took a huge bite out of it.

"I thought only kids went through phases," I said, grabbing the rest of my sandwich and starting to eat it, too. Lillian had made my favorite—peanut butter and honey.

"Why were you staring a hole in the wall when I came over?" River mumbled between chews.

"It's very restful," I informed her. I thought about telling her about Maria and my plan. River would be a good recruit, since she lived in Walcott Corners. "I have this problem."

River swallowed her food, took another sip of milk and pushed her tray away. "Boy, are you lucky I ran into you. You're talking to exactly the right person. I'm studying to be a pop psychologist, you know — just like my mom. People pay her to listen to their problems and she helps them out. I've helped just about everybody in this school already — except for Anna Banana. She's beyond help. I won't even charge you, since this is a first visit."

I looked River up and down for a few seconds. She really did seem more okay than when I'd met her. In fact, she seemed a little unusual. I liked that in a person. "It's not that kind of a problem."

"Oh, well, that's okay. I'm sure whatever it is, we can take care of it." River added, "That's the first rule of being a pop psychologist — sympathize with the patient."

"My problem is you," I confessed. "I have a proposition for you."

River listened to me talk about the first stage of my plan for bringing down Walcott Corners and forgot all about being sympathetic. Before I could even ask if she wanted to help, she interrupted me and said, "Count me in."

I smiled again. River wasn't so bad. Once you got used to her blunt way of speaking, she was actually kind of cool.

"You really get people to pay you to give them advice?" I stood up with River as the bell rang. Lunch period was over and we both had music class together next.

"Mm-hmm," she replied as we walked toward the huge gray garbage cans standing in the middle of the cafeteria.

"Can I ask you a question?" I said seriously.

"Fire away." River dumped everything into the garbage can, including her tray.

"How can I get in on that?"

•　　•　　•

"Welcome aboard, Just Ola." Mr. Elijah was grinning so wide I could see all of his teeth. He opened the door to his house all the way. "Come on in."

"I can't, Mr. Elijah. I just wanted to make sure it was okay to use your house to meet with all the kids in the neighborhood tonight," I said, smiling. River and I had talked to all of the kids on the bus who lived in Walcott Corners, and we'd gotten sixteen other kids to join us. Mr. Elijah had been right. When we told them about getting all the rules changed about where to play, curfews, and riding bikes on the sidewalk, everybody had wanted to join in. This neighborhood had just been waiting for someone to come and lead them.

"Glad to oblige," Mr. Elijah said. "Then you and I can talk, 'cause we're gonna have to coordinate our efforts."

"Right, Mr. Elijah. See you later." I turned and started walking toward my house. I had some work to do. I had to come up with a really good plan to shake this neighborhood up. I had to make things—

I stopped. I could hear the sound of wailing coming from somewhere. I turned to look at Otis's house. Yup. It was Davis screaming from somewhere on the second floor of the house. I turned all the way around and crossed the street. Before I started making my big plans, there was one little thing that I needed to take care of.

I knocked on Otis's door as loud as I could. Aeisha and Otis were probably in there trying one of their stupid new ideas on poor Davis. I knew I could get that baby to sleep and help poor Otis's mama. Then maybe she would start taking care of Otis. I couldn't have my sister's boyfriend going around looking like such a mess.

146

Mrs. Spunklemeyer opened the door. She was wearing the same long bathrobe she'd worn when she brought us the pumpkin pie. She probably hadn't changed out of it since the baby was born. "Hello. You're Ola, Aeisha's sister."

I nodded. "I came to help them with the baby."

Mrs. Spunklemeyer sniffed. "Come in, Ola. Otis and Aeisha are upstairs trying to get Davis to sleep now. They said something about trying to find what kind of music he liked."

I walked in. "You go lie down, Mrs. Spunklemeyer. I'll go take care of Davis. I used to help Mrs. Gransby baby-sit all her grandchildren, you know."

I marched up the stairs. I could hear rock music floating from somewhere upstairs, then what sounded like country music. I followed the sound of the music to the baby's room, and there were Aeisha and Otis, standing over the crib with a portable radio.

"You guys don't know what you're doing," I said, pushing past them. I looked down into the crib. There was a fat pink baby with Otis's stick-up hair, bawling. Davis. I reached out and tickled the bottom of his feet.

Davis stopped crying long enough to look at me with surprise.

"Works every time," I whispered to Aeisha and Otis. I picked up one of Davis's feet and started rubbing the bottom softly. Mrs. Gransby had taught me that babies love to have their feet massaged.

"What do you know?" Otis whispered in amazement as Davis's eyes started to close. "Thanks, Ola."

Aeisha looked at me, surprised. I could tell she was im-

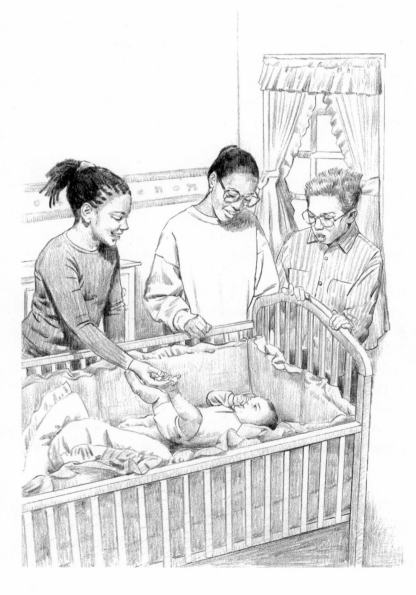

pressed. She would know this trick, too, if she'd spent less time reading when we were at Mrs. Gransby's house after school. "Yeah, thanks."

I shrugged and put Davis's foot down. He was fast asleep. "Don't forget about the meeting later on. See ya."

I didn't see Mrs. Spunklemeyer downstairs as I left the house, but I figured she'd gone upstairs and gone to bed. I started humming to myself as I crossed the street.

> *I wanna shake it up,*
>   *shake it up,*
>   *shake it up*
> *Like an earthquake. . . .*

I smiled when I realized that I was humming the last part to my special jump-rope song. Just thinking the words put me in a better mood than I'd been in since we moved here. I went into the house and found Grady waiting for me inside the hallway, but I just gave him a pat and called out hello to Lillian before going upstairs to my room. I had some serious planning to do. I sat down at my desk and pulled out a sheet of paper and a pen. The way I figured it, what this neighborhood needed was a little bit of Roxbury—actually, a whole lot of Roxbury. I started writing a list of all the things I had loved about my old neighborhood.

Chapter Eleven

Operation Shake It Up

I stood outside the big oak door of Maria's house nervously. It was the day of the big town meeting, and I had ridden my bike over to Maria's house in the middle of town to check on her before she left for the meeting. Everybody in town was gonna be at that meeting except for the kids and senior citizens from Walcott Corners. While Maria was submitting our petition and talking about all that revenue stuff, we would be back in Walcott Corners transforming the neighborhood.

Maria opened the door and pulled me inside quickly. "Keep it quiet. My mother and sisters are upstairs."

"I thought you were supposed to dress up for this meeting," I said, whispering.

"I did dress up." Maria pointed to her new bandanna, which was a bright orange and blue. "What's the matter with you?"

I stopped shuffling my feet and stood still. "I'm nervous. Here are the petitions. You gonna be okay?"

"Piece of cake." Maria nodded confidently. "I came up with some great plans to generate alternative revenue. My dad helped me put together a cost estimate, even. He promised not to tell Mom, so she's gonna be in for a big shock when I get up at the meeting." Maria looked really pleased at the idea of upsetting her mother.

"So you'll call me when the meeting's over, right?" I asked. "And you'll come over? Don't forget to bring your bike."

Maria smiled. "Don't worry about it, Ola. It's all under control. Are you ready?"

I grinned. "You bet."

I biked home as fast as I could. Our house was empty except for Lillian and Grady. I had talked Mama and Dad into letting me stay home from the meeting by telling them River had invited me over to her house for lunch. They were so pleased that I was finally making friends that they couldn't say no. But Aeisha had to go with them or it would look suspicious. I parked my bike on our lawn and looked around the neighborhood. Immaculate square lawns, big houses, vacant streets. I hoped this was the last time Walcott Corners would look so empty to me.

I dashed in the house. The phone was ringing already. I knew it was Mr. Elijah calling to check with me.

"Just Ola? Are we A-OK on stage one?" Mr. Elijah's voice sounded merry.

"Roger, Mr. Elijah. Set stage one into motion," I ordered, trying to sound serious. I had a surprise for Mr. Elijah and I didn't want to give it away. As soon as the seniors at Walcott finished stage one, I could get all the kids into action. I hung up with Mr. Elijah and called River to tell her it was okay to come over. Then I headed into the kitchen to check on Lillian.

I could smell all the delicious food cooking before I even entered the kitchen. Lillian was at the stove minding three big kettles of food. I had asked Lillian to make some special food from her country. A lot of the seniors in the neighborhood were doing the same thing. I pulled a chair over to the stove and stood up on it so I could look into the kettles. "Whatcha making, Lillian?"

Lillian took the lid off one of the kettles and stirred a thick green stew. I could see potatoes, dumplings, and plantains in it, but then Lillian stirred some more and I saw that there were crabs in it, too. "This one *calalou.*"

"What's in the other ones?"

Lillian took the lids off the other pots, and I saw that there was black rice and shrimp in one pot and pieces of braised pork in the other one. *"Du riz djon-djon. Griot."*

"Is your friend coming, too?" I inhaled deeply. The delicious odors coming from the pots made my stomach growl.

"Yes, Sonja is coming." Lillian smiled and nodded. Sonja was her friend from English class. "She making bread. She say six loaves."

"Wow." I looked down at the food again. My stomach was rumbling even louder now. "Can I have some?"

"No. Is for later." Lillian said sternly.

"But Lillian—" I was cut off by the sound of the doorbell. "That must be River. I'll be right back. It's time to let Grady out, too." I ran into the hallway, the dog right behind me.

"You know what to do, right, Grady?" I stood in front of the door for a moment and patted his head. "It's real easy. Just be a dog."

Grady barked, and I checked one more time to make sure he had his ID tags on his collar. Then I opened the door. "Grady's all ready, River. . . ."

My voice trailed off. It wasn't River at the front door.

"Well, Ola, did we knock the wind out of you?" Mrs. Gransby said, smiling down at me.

I looked from Mrs. Gransby to Karen and Margarita and then back to Mrs. Gransby, but all I could think to say was, "Omigosh."

"She doesn't look happy to see us," Margarita said flatly. "We can go, you know."

"That's not it," Karen said, smiling. "She's up to something, I can tell."

"Mrs. Gransby." I wrapped my arms around her stomach and gave her a big hug.

Mrs. Gransby patted my head with her soft hands and tugged at my braids. "Ola, you get so big, my shoes soon fit you."

"What are you guys doing here?" I let go of Mrs. Gransby and stood awkwardly in front of Karen and Margarita. I hadn't spoken to them in weeks, and I hoped they weren't mad at me.

"We're here to surprise you," Margarita answered. She was sulking. That was just like Margarita. "But I still say you don't look happy. You're still mad at us, aren't you?"

"I'm not mad at you." I stepped back and shook my head.

"You haven't called us in three weeks," Karen chimed in.

"I tried to call you a couple of times, but you were never home."

"I'd love to see inside this house," Mrs. Gransby murmured, "before the cold make my nose drop off."

I stepped to the side. I was still in shock. I was happy to see Mrs. Gransby, Margarita and Karen, but why did they have to pick *now* to come and visit? "I'm sorry, Mrs. Gransby. You all come inside."

"I ask my eyes if they seeing real when the taxicar stop here, Ola," Mrs. Gransby said, walking in and looking around. "I never did see such a house before."

"It's not that unusual, Mrs. Gransby. There are seven more houses on the street just like it." Before I closed the door, I stuck my head outside and looked around. Stage one of Operation Shake It Up was well on its way. I could already see four cars parked on the street. I remembered Grady and grabbed his collar to push him outside. "Go, boy."

Then I shut the door and turned around. Margarita, Karen and Mrs. Gransby were staring at me as they took off their hats and coats. "Come on into the living room."

"What are you up to now, Ola?" Karen asked, following me.

"This house is huuuuuge," Margarita said. She went to look out of the picture window. "It's much bigger than the house we found for you."

"You found me a house?" I said, plopping down in one of the armchairs. I had forgotten to have Margarita and Karen call off the house search.

Karen nodded. "It's on Redman Street, but that's only two

blocks away from your old street. It's got four bedrooms . . . but you don't want it anymore, do you?"

I looked down at my feet. "A lot's happened, you guys."

"Well, that's why we're here, Ola," Mrs. Gransby said seriously. "Margarita and Karen came over to see me the other day, and their long faces and sad eyes tell me it's high time for to come visit you and see what's happened to you."

I kept my eyes trained on my feet. "I guess I'm not coming back to the old neighborhood."

"See, I told you. She doesn't care about us anymore." Margarita threw herself down on the couch and flipped her hair back with a big sigh. I almost smiled, 'cause I realized how much I had really missed Margarita and all her drama.

"I thought you didn't like it here." Karen sat down beside Margarita and leaned back against the cushions. "You made this place sound like a dungeon."

"It doesn't have anything to do with you guys," I said earnestly. "I miss you guys a lot. I wasn't calling 'cause I figured you had forgotten about me."

"No way." Karen shook her head, and I noticed that her hair was longer and that she seemed to have more freckles on her face. "School is so boring without you around to shake things up."

"This place isn't so bad," I admitted finally. "It turns out they need somebody like me. Mama and Dad like their new jobs."

"What about us?" Margarita asked seriously.

I got up out of the armchair and went to sit next to them on the couch. "I promise to keep calling."

"You have to come and visit, too," Karen said, pulling a

piece of paper from her pocket. "We made a list of things you have to do just in case you weren't coming back. You have to write to us once a week."

"And one of us has to come visit the other once a month. It's only three hours away," Margarita added. "We took this bus that even showed a movie on it."

"Okay," I promised without even looking at the list. I was glad Margarita and Karen were here.

"Ola," Mrs. Gransby called. I looked and saw that she was peering out the picture window. "I do believe you have some visitors coming. A whole troop of visitors."

"I knew you were up to something," Karen said with a laugh.

"Something big." I stood up. "And I could really use your help."

Karen and Margarita looked at each other and then back at me. They nodded together. "What do you want us to do?"

I could hear the sound of all the neighborhood kids outside the house. River must have gathered everyone together.

"Karen, you know those super-cool hopscotch squares you used to draw? You gotta organize that. And I need you to supervise all the games, Margarita—'cause you always remember all the rules." I went over to the window and grabbed Mrs. Gransby's hand. "And could you open the door? I gotta introduce Mrs. Gransby to Lillian."

"This looks great," River said, smiling. "But boy, are you gonna be in big trouble."

I looked around at the neighborhood again. Maybe we

had overdone it a little. It looked so different. Mr. Elijah had organized all the seniors to move their cars out of the driveways and into the street in clear violation of rule number two of the neighborhood association. As for other rules we had broken, neighbors were sitting on the chairs we had set up on the lawns and the sidewalks. There were tables with all sorts of food lining the sidewalk, and bikes and toys littering the lawns. Karen had everyone draw her special hopscotch squares on all the driveways in three different colors of chalk, and Margarita had organized jump rope, freeze tag and even a baseball game at the end of the block. I could hear the kids playing jump rope chanting, "Shake it up, shake it up." Besides that, there were dogs and kids running loose all over the neighborhood. Every once in a while I would catch sight of Grady chasing another dog across the street or around some house. He was following my instructions and acting like a dog. Later on, Lillian would be putting on a show where he was the main attraction.

But that wasn't all. With the help of Mr. Julius Jones, I had rigged up the longest clothesline in the world. It stretched from the front of my house all the way across the street to Otis's house. All the kids on the street had donated different-colored T-shirts to hang up on it, and we had spelled out WELCOME TO THE NEW WALCOTT CORNERS: AN UNCOOPERATIVE NEIGHBORHOOD across the shirts in different-colored markers. Mr. Elijah had been really pleased to see his son-in-law helping us.

Looking around, I realized that it still didn't look much like Roxbury — but it definitely looked better than it had. The best part was that everybody was having fun.

157

"Mr. and Mrs. Stern are gonna have a fit," River added, sniffling.

I handed her a tissue from the box I was carrying. That had been Mrs. Gransby's idea. It was too cold to be having a block party, but no one seemed to mind that much. "Here come more people."

I pointed down the street to where some more cars had stopped. There was no room on the street to drive. Maria Poncinelli flew past the cars on her bike with a huge grin on her face. Then I saw Mama and Dad picking their way through the street toward me. "Uh-oh."

I looked around for someplace to hide. From the looks on Mama and Dad's faces, no one needed to tell them I was responsible for this whole plan.

"You can't run away from your problems, Ola." River nodded wisely. From the tone of her voice, I knew she was giving me some of her pop psychology. "You gotta face them head-on."

I took a deep breath. River was right. I looked at Mama and Dad again and gulped.

Maria reached me first. She screeched to a stop right beside River and me and jumped off her bike. "We won!"

"All right!" I forgot all about Mama and Dad for a second as I jumped up and down with Maria and River. Maria was so excited, she couldn't even act cool anymore. Then I heard Dad's voice.

"Ayeola!"

I turned around. He and Mama were standing right behind me with mad looks on their faces. I heard River and Maria scoot away quickly.

I tried to smile. "Hi, Mama. Hi, Dad."

Mama waved her arms in the direction of the clothes-lines, the games and the food. "What in the world . . . ?"

"We don't even have to ask if this was your idea." Dad sighed. He looked really disappointed.

I hung my head. "Most of it."

"Where is Lillian?" Mama asked, looking around.

I looked up. "She's setting up for the dog show with Grady. But she didn't have anything to do with this. It was all me."

Dad nodded. "Well, it looks great."

He and Mama were smiling at me now.

"Heyyy . . . ," I began.

All of a sudden Mama and Dad broke out into big smiles, like they couldn't pretend to be mad anymore. "I can't tell you how glad I am to see you acting like your old self again." Mama grabbed me into a big hug. "I was worried our girl had gone away forever."

"You don't mind that I did all this?" I asked, hugging Mama back.

"Ola, child, I'll tell you a secret." Mama smiled. "I never did like all those rules about living here."

"A person should be able to mow his lawn when *he* wants to," Dad grumbled, putting his hand on my head and stroking it. "And park his car in front of his own house, and have visitors as late as he wants and— Is that Mrs. Gransby jumping in those leaves over there?"

I nodded. "It's a long story, Dad."

"Khatib." I knocked on his door softly. It was late and I was supposed to have been asleep hours earlier. But all my thoughts about what had happened that day and the family and moving here had kept me awake. Everything had gone perfect. Maria had won her fight at the town meeting. The town had agreed to reconsider the designs of the new houses for the other development, and she had gotten them to vote yes on disbanding the neighborhood association. She even told me that her mom said she did a good job. I knew her grandmother would have been proud of her, too.

"Who is it?" Khatib's voice sounded out of breath, like I had caught him in the middle of something.

"It's me, Ola. Let me in," I ordered in a whisper.

I heard a noise that sounded like Khatib moving around. Whatever he was doing, he didn't want me to see. A few seconds later he called out, "Come in," in his regular voice.

I opened the door and slid into the room, looking around slowly. It looked normal. Khatib was lying on his bed reading a sports magazine, and his room was in its usual state of disaster, with clothes, music tapes and shoes all over the floor. His schoolbooks were piled up on top of each other on the desk, and his bed wasn't made. Mama makes him clean his room every Friday, but by the next morning it's back in the same condition it was in before.

I sat down on the edge of the bed and looked around more carefully. I was looking for clues as to what Khatib had been doing. Whenever Aeisha tried to hide something from me in a hurry, she stuck it under her pillow or under her bed. That's how I'd discovered that she'd bought some red lipstick the week before. But Khatib didn't look like he had anything under his pillows. In fact, his pillow was on the floor. I looked around at the edge of the bed.

161

"What are you looking for, Ola?" Khatib asked. His eyes were zeroed in on me.

"Nothing." I picked at a small hole in my jeans.

"What do you want?" Khatib leaned forward a little, and I saw that he was wearing a black-and-gold Walcott College sweatshirt. Mama had given all three of us sweatshirts during her first week of work. I also noticed that he was holding his magazine upside down. Ah-ha! Oldest mistake in the book. Now I knew he had been hiding something. "You need to talk about something?"

"Yeah." I nodded, looking at his face.

"What's your problem?" Khatib asked, leaning back against the wood headboard of his bed. He was starting to look worried about my being so quiet. "Mama and Dad aren't mad at you, right?"

I shook my head.

"Aeisha?" Khatib asked.

"Mama and Dad are mad at her." I smiled. Aeisha had told Mama and Dad about her science grade earlier that night and they had gotten all upset. They said that they didn't need her to try and get proof that Mr. Stillwell was grading her unfairly. They would have believed her and done something about it if she had just told them. It was nice having Mama and Dad mad at someone else in this family besides me.

"Things okay with Karen and Margarita?"

I nodded. Karen, Margarita and Mrs. Gransby had stayed for dinner and then gone home on the late bus. I had been sorry to see them leave, but I knew that I would see them again soon. I planned to follow everything on Karen and Margarita's list, and I'd made them promise to come back during Christmas vacation for a real visit. I had given Mrs. Gransby an extra-long hug. Even though we lived so far apart, her bringing Karen and Margarita to see me showed that she was still looking after me.

"Then what?"

"It's you," I spoke up finally. "Did you quit the basketball team?"

Khatib dropped his eyes for a second. "I knew you would figure it out. I should have carried my gym bag out with me."

"Yeah. You gave yourself away big-time." I moved up the bed to sit next to him, stretching my legs out beside his. There was no way I was going to let him know that I had followed him to his dance class. "So how come you quit the team?"

Khatib shrugged. "It just wasn't the same here."

"Nothing's the same here," I agreed. "But I thought you loved basketball."

"I used to love it — before I had to play it so much." Khatib nudged me with his shoulder. "Back in the old neighborhood, everybody thought I should play, just 'cause I was tall and I was good at it. And I didn't mind playing when it was just around the neighborhood and it was just for fun. Then when high school started, everybody was saying, 'Hey, Khatib — you trying out for the team?' It was like I had to do it."

"You didn't like playing on the team?" I was surprised.

"It was okay sometimes. The best part was winning all those games and having everybody look up to me," Khatib admitted. "It kinda went to my head a little."

I bit my lip to keep myself from saying something flip. Khatib and I were having a serious talk for once, and I didn't want to destroy the mood and get kicked out of his room.

"But those drills, the practice every day and Saturday . . . I could skip all that," Khatib continued.

"That's why you quit the team here?" I turned my head to look at him. "Why didn't you quit at our old school?"

Khatib hesitated.

"It wasn't 'cause of what those guys on the team said about you that first day?" I asked.

Khatib pursed his lips. "That was part of it. My heart wasn't in being on the team anyway. I tried out 'cause Dad made all those special arrangements to get me a tryout. But when I heard the kind of stuff this one guy was saying, I was, like, forget this. I'm not putting up with this for something I'm not even that crazy about. I got better things to do."

Like dance class? I wanted to ask him, but I already knew the answer. Khatib had found something he was more interested in than basketball. "You don't miss playing basketball? For real, Khatib?"

"I miss shooting hoops with Dad. I haven't used the one in the back 'cause I knew he'd be able to tell I wasn't practicing," Khatib admitted softly. His breath tickled my ear as he turned to talk to me.

"And you don't care what those guys on the basketball team said about you?" I asked anxiously.

"It was only one guy. And he was stupid, Ola. He thought I was gonna take his place on the team. Besides, I heard that kind of stuff all the time when we played against white teams at the old school. That's not what was important.

What was important was how I felt about basketball," Khatib said firmly.

I nodded. I felt a lot better now. Khatib had been the only thing that I was still worried about. I couldn't get over the change in him. He had been acting a lot less conceited lately.

And Aeisha was falling in love. I still thought that was gross, but I could handle it. Dad was getting used to the pressures of his new job and was making an effort to be home more. Then there was Lillian. At dinner that night, she had talked and laughed as much as the rest of us. She had two families now—one in Haiti and one here with us.

I pulled my knees up. "Why haven't you told Mama and Dad?"

"I will." Khatib fixed his eyes on me. "When I'm ready. You can't tell them, Ola. Promise."

"What?" I asked innocently.

"Promise, Ola," Khatib repeated. His eyes bounced back and forth from my hands to my face. He wanted to make sure I wasn't going to cross my fingers behind my back or cheat in some other way.

"Promise what?"

"Ola."

"I promise," I said, standing up. "Thanks, Khatib. And you know what?"

"What?"

I opened the door and started backing out of the room carefully. "I won't tell them about your dance lessons, either."

I was back in my room before Khatib had a chance to

close his mouth. I climbed into bed and pulled the covers up over my head. I listened carefully. I could just make out the sound of the jazz station coming from Mama and Dad's radio, but there was something else, too. It was the sound of someone humming. I realized I could hear Lillian in her room next door. Aeisha was in her room reading, and Khatib was practicing his dancing. I closed my eyes. This house was finally starting to feel right.

About the Author

Joanne Hyppolite is the author of *Seth and Samona,* winner of the second annual Marguerite de Angeli Prize, given by Delacorte Press for a first novel for middle-grade readers. She was born in Haiti and came to live in the United States when she was four years old. She grew up in Dorchester, Massachusetts. Joanne Hyppolite graduated from the University of Pennsylvania with a degree in creative writing and received her master's degree from the department of Afro-American Studies at the University of California, Los Angeles. She lives in Florida, where she is a graduate student at the University of Miami.